PRAISE FOR **squish!**

"Even the mildest young boy will see something of himself in Squish. *Super Amoeba* is an energetic, good-hearted escapade, one that young readers will enjoy."
—*The New York Times*

★ "The hilarious misadventures of a hapless young everylad who happens to be an amoeba. If ever a new series deserved to go viral, this one does."
—*Kirkus Reviews*, Starred

"The Holms strike a breezy, goofy tone right out of the gate."
—*Publishers Weekly*

"A perfect mix of writing that is simple enough for early readers but still remarkably snarky, clever, and entertaining. . . . Kids themselves will soak up the humor, tidbits of science instruction, and adventure."
—*The Bulletin of the Center for Children's Books*

"A new graphic novel series that will have readers everywhere clapping their pseudopods in glee. There's some real science worked in here too and even directions for a kid-friendly experiment."
—*Bookends* (*Booklist* blog)

Read ALL the SQUISH books!

#1 SQUISH: Super Amoeba
#2 SQUISH: Brave New Pond
#3 SQUISH: The Power of the Parasite
#4 SQUISH: Captain Disaster
#5 SQUISH: Game On!

squish
GAME ON!

BY JENNIFER L. HOLM & MATTHEW HOLM

RANDOM HOUSE NEW YORK

Copyright © 2013 by Jennifer Holm and Matthew Holm

All rights reserved. Published in the United States by Random House Children's Books, a division of Random House, Inc., New York.

Random House and the colophon are registered trademarks of Random House, Inc.

Visit us on the Web! randomhouse.com/kids

Educators and librarians, for a variety of teaching tools, visit us at RHTeachersLibrarians.com

Library of Congress Cataloging-in-Publication Data
Holm, Jennifer L.
Game on! / by Jennifer L. Holm & Matthew Holm. —
1st ed.   p.   cm. — (Squish ; #5)
Summary: Squish the amoeba neglects his homework, parents, friends, and even his Super Amoeba comic books when he discovers the video game Mitosis.
ISBN 978-0-307-98299-5 (trade) —
ISBN 978-0-307-98300-8 (lib. bdg.) —
ISBN 978-0-307-98301-5 (ebook)
1. Graphic novels. [1. Graphic novels. 2. Amoeba—Fiction.
3. Video games—Fiction. 4. Cartoons and comics—Fiction.
5. Superheroes—Fiction.] I. Holm, Matthew. II. Title.
PZ7.7.H65Gam 2013 741.5'973—dc23 2012016421

MANUFACTURED IN MALAYSIA 10 9 8 7 6 5 4 3 2
First Edition

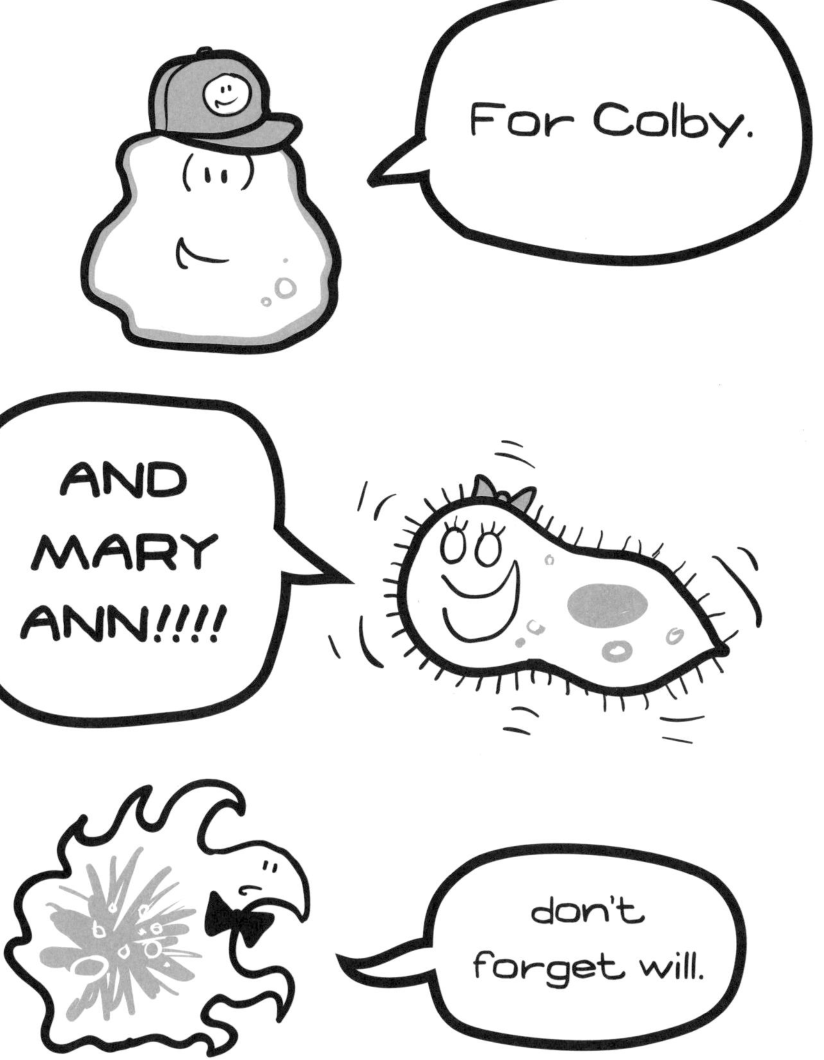
For Colby.
AND MARY ANN!!!!
don't forget will.

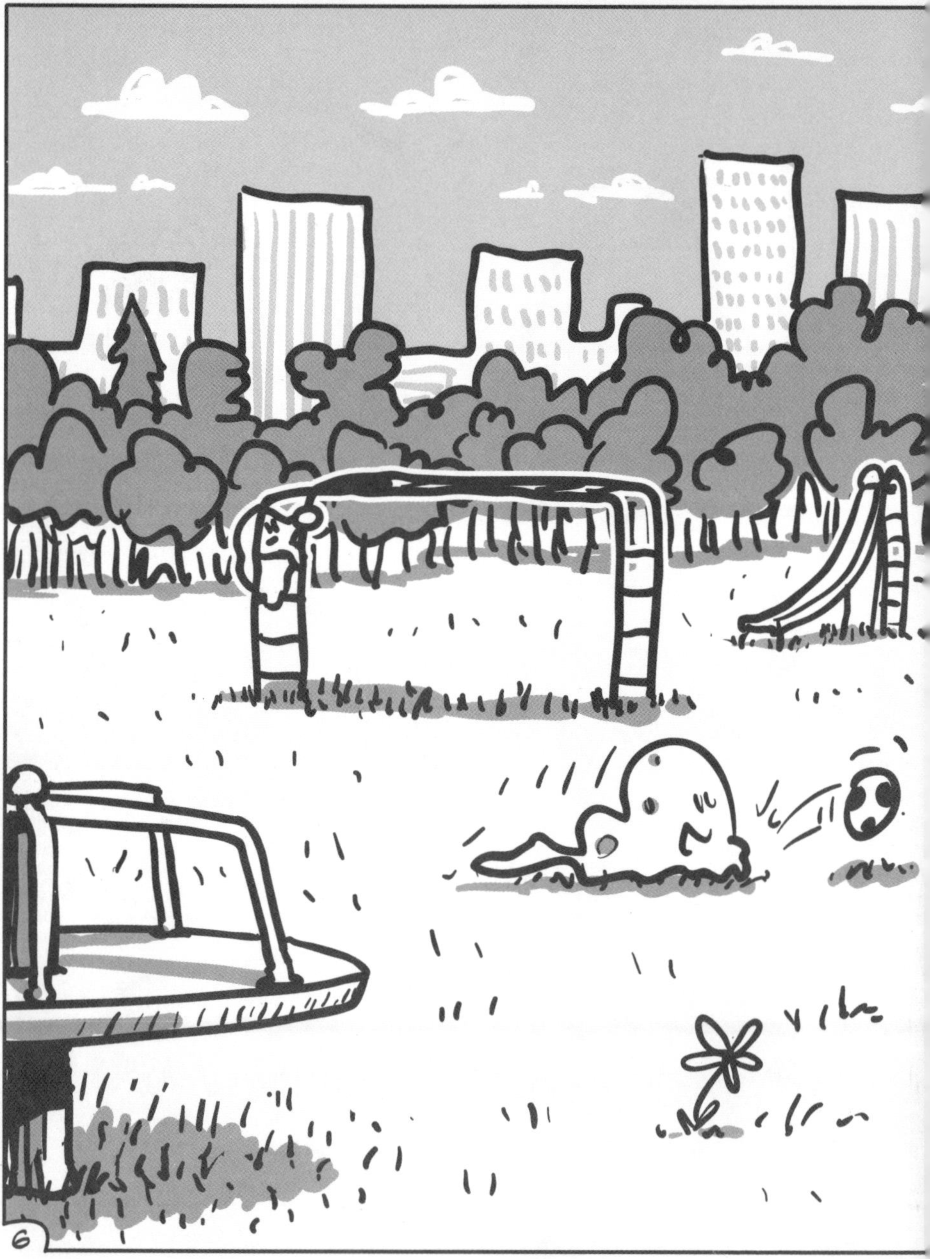

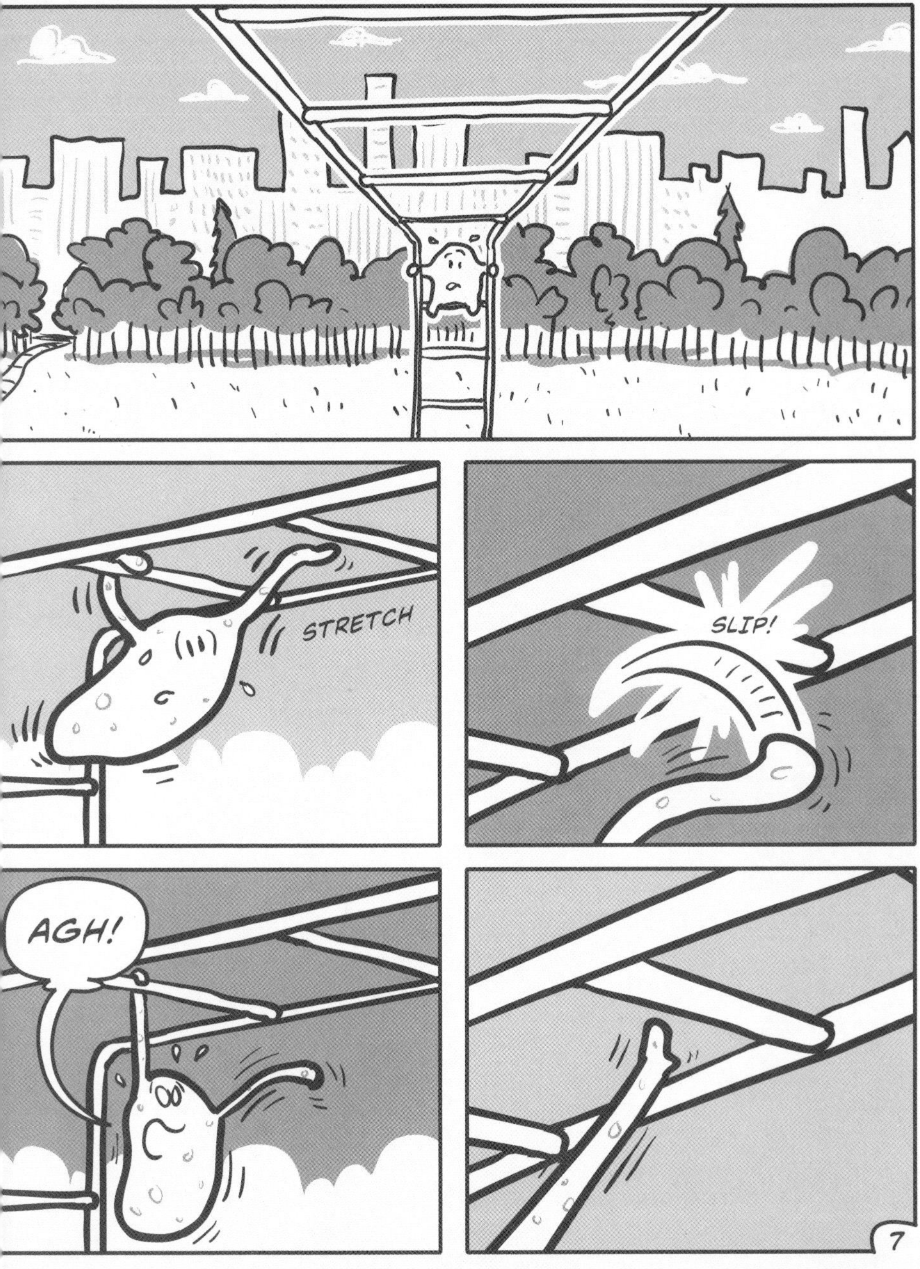
STRETCH
SLIP!
AGH!

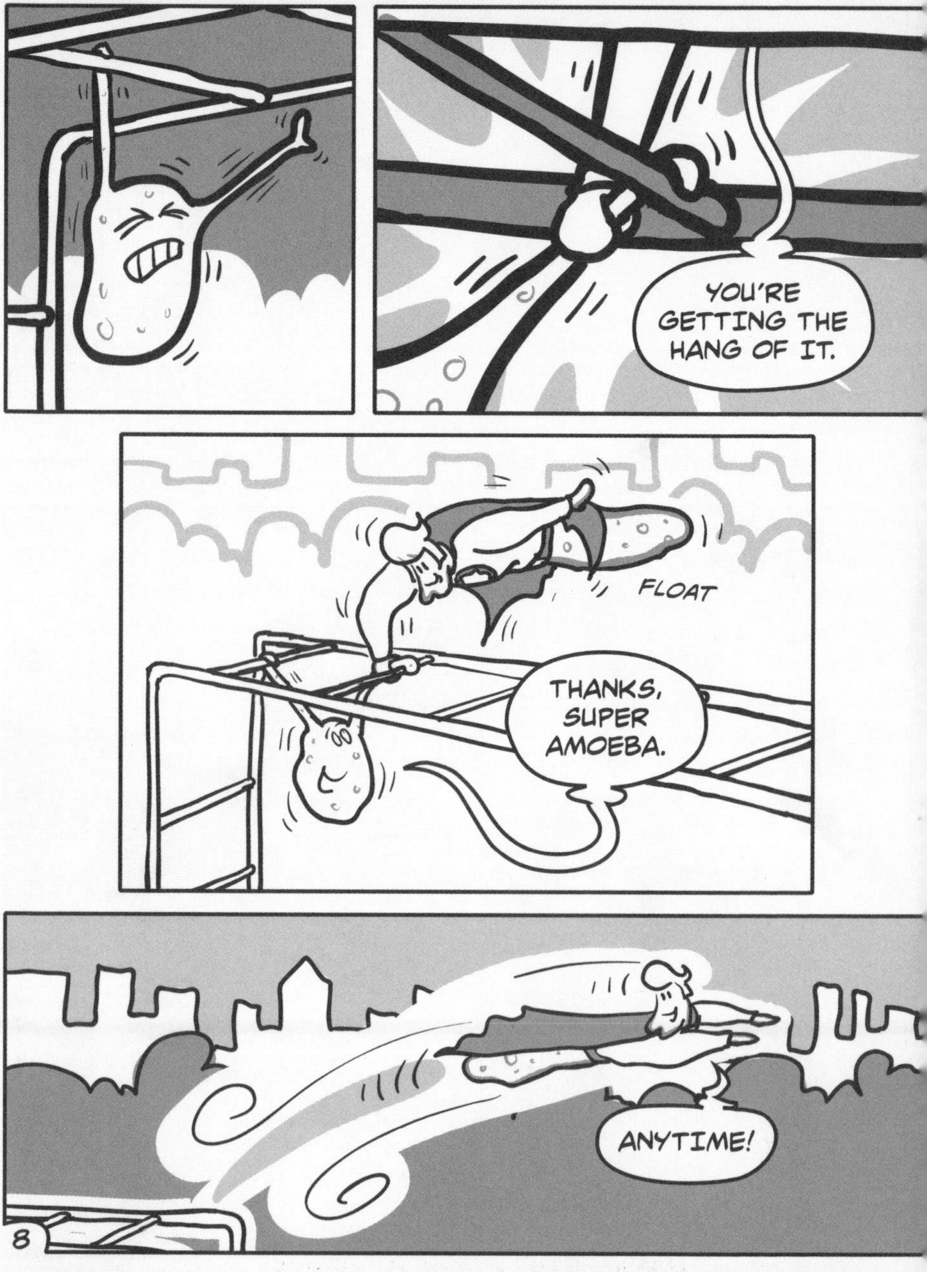
YOU'RE GETTING THE HANG OF IT.
FLOAT
THANKS, SUPER AMOEBA.
ANYTIME!

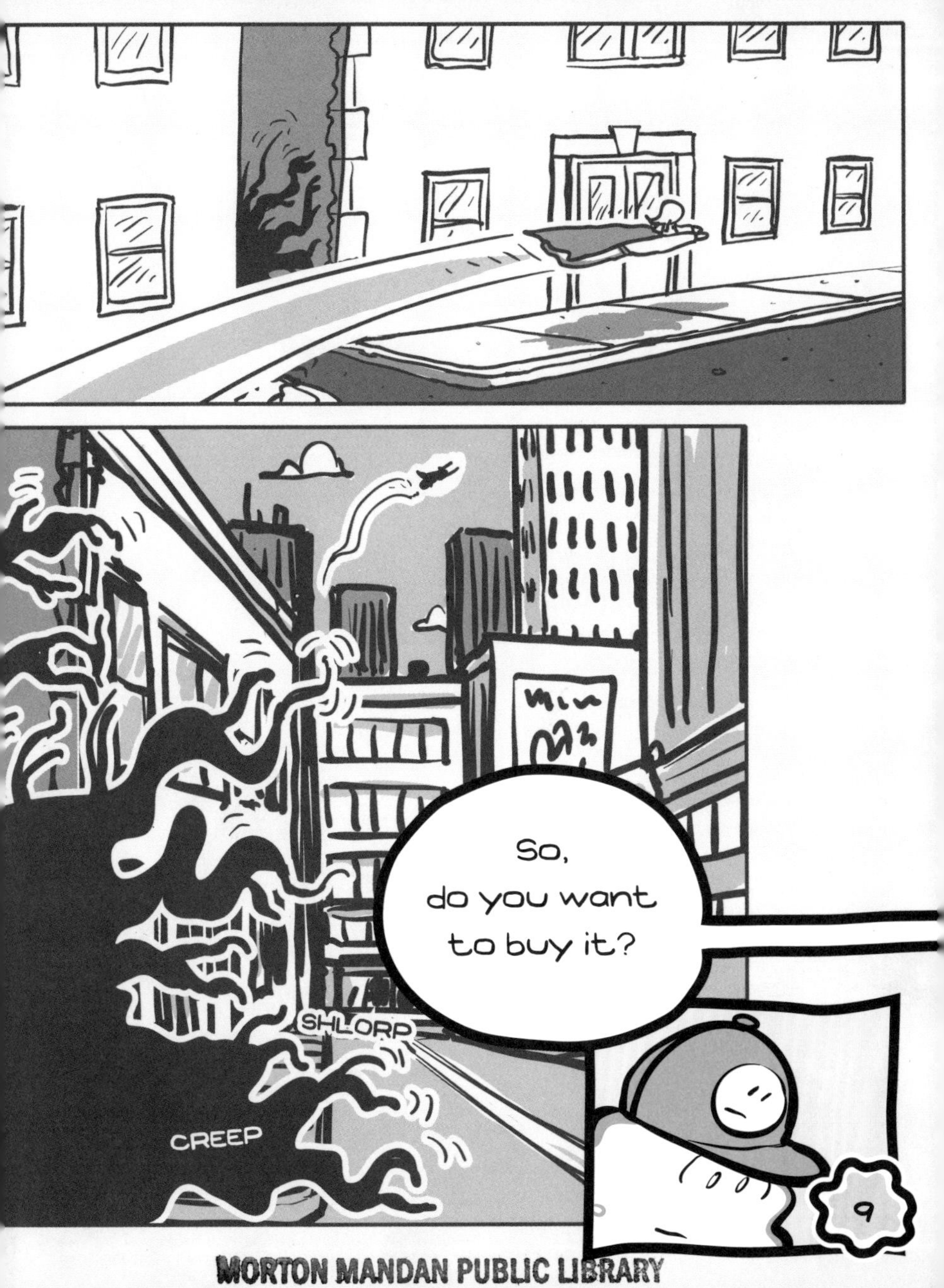
So,
do you want
to buy it?
SHLORP
CREEP
9

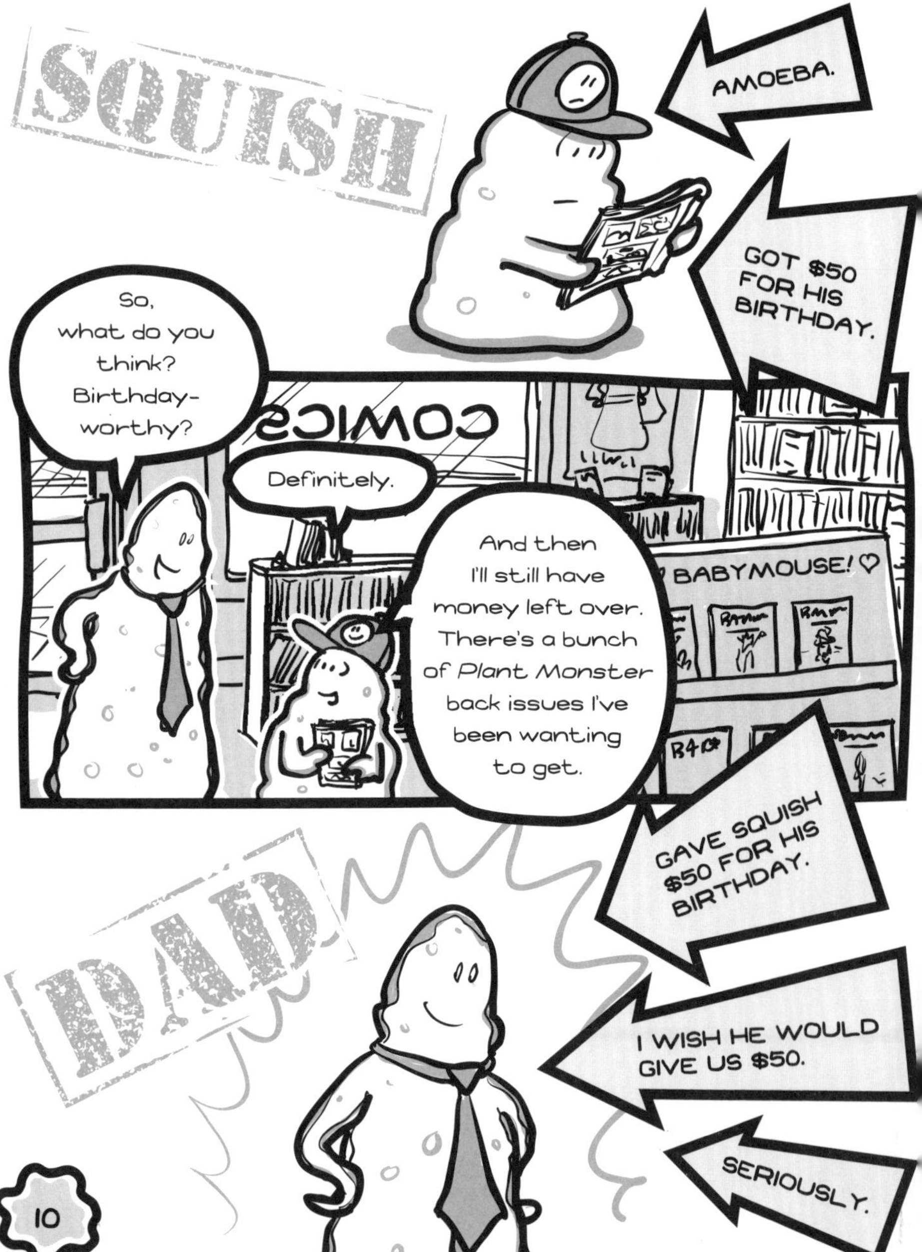
SQUISH
AMOEBA.
GOT $50 FOR HIS BIRTHDAY.
So, what do you think? Birthday-worthy?
COMICS
Definitely.
And then I'll still have money left over. There's a bunch of *Plant Monster* back issues I've been wanting to get.
♡ BABYMOUSE! ♡
DAD
GAVE SQUISH $50 FOR HIS BIRTHDAY.
I WISH HE WOULD GIVE US $50.
SERIOUSLY.

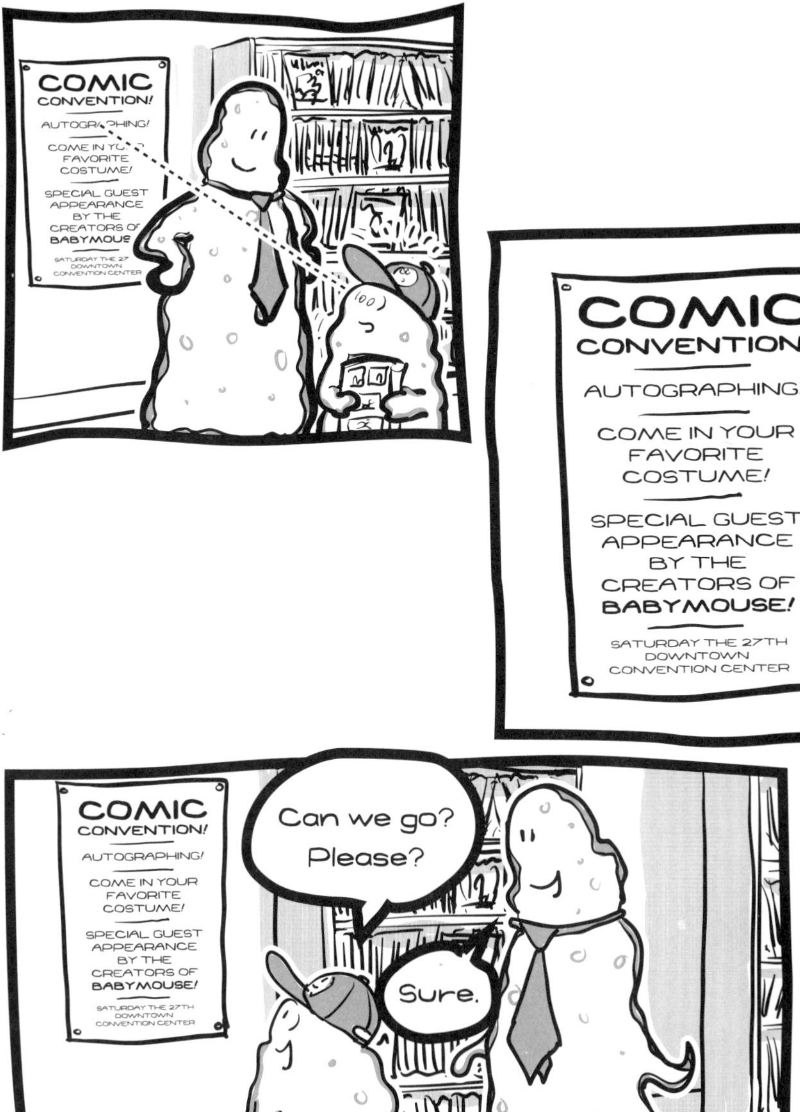
COMIC CONVENTION!
AUTOGRAPHING!
COME IN YOUR FAVORITE COSTUME!
SPECIAL GUEST APPEARANCE BY THE CREATORS OF BABYMOUSE!
SATURDAY THE 27TH DOWNTOWN CONVENTION CENTER
Can we go? Please?
Sure.

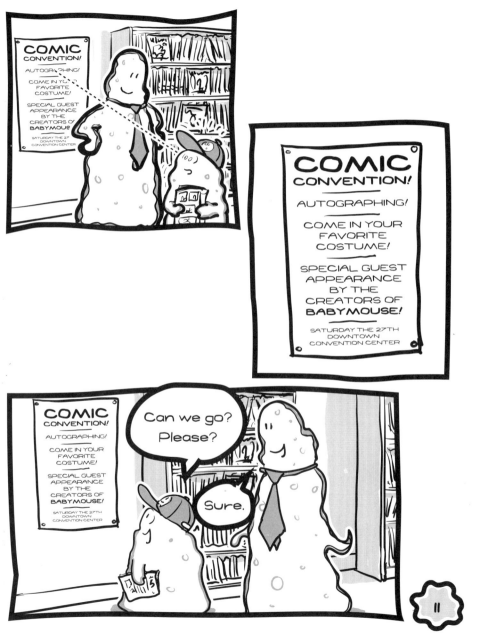

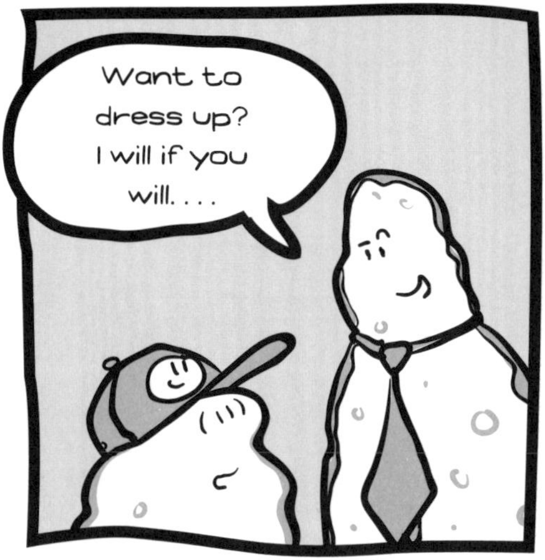
Want to dress up? I will if you will. . . .

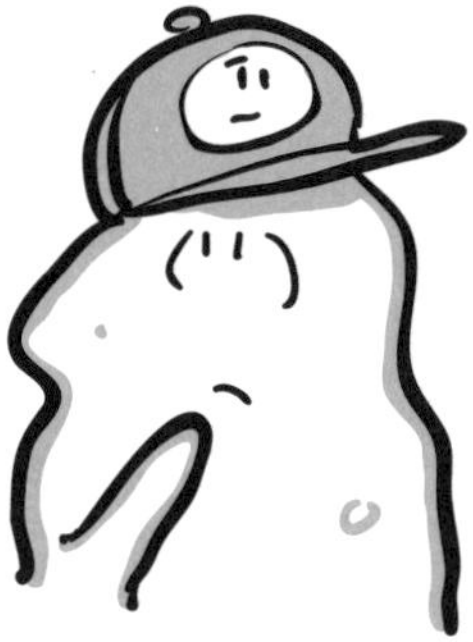

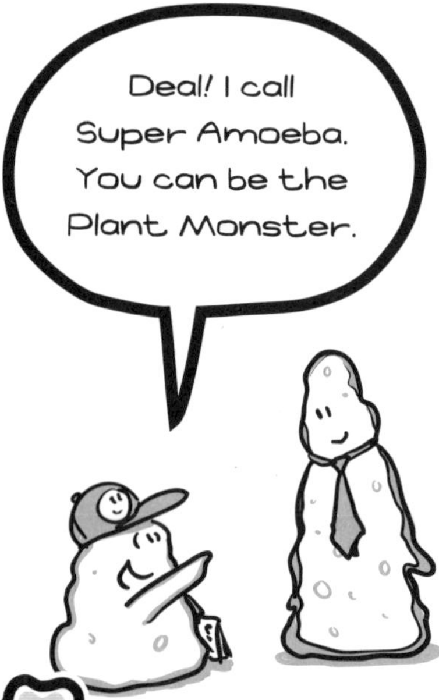
Deal! I call Super Amoeba. You can be the Plant Monster.

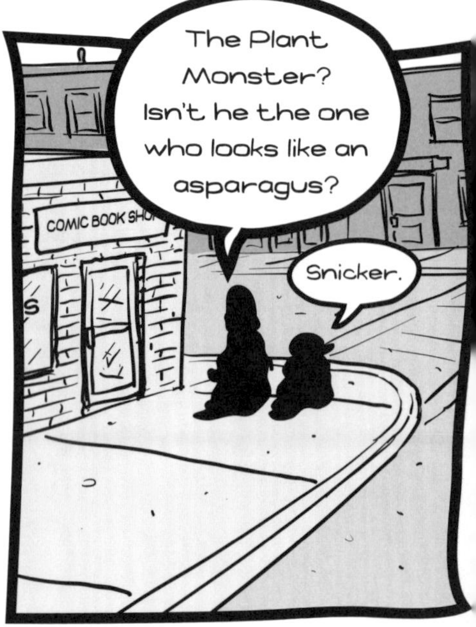
The Plant Monster? Isn't he the one who looks like an asparagus?
Snicker.
COMIC BOOK SHO

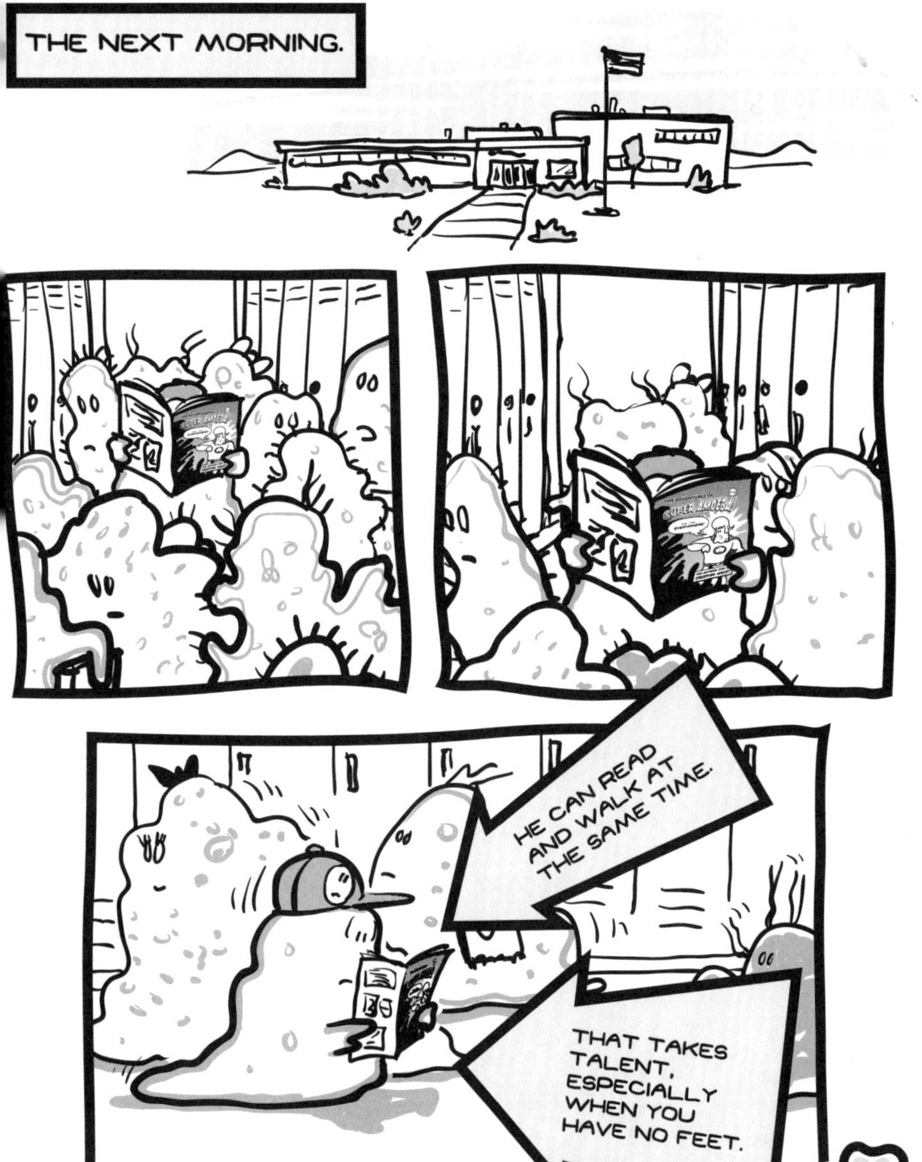
THE NEXT MORNING.
THE ADVENTURES OF
SUPER AMOEBA!
HE CAN READ AND WALK AT THE SAME TIME.
THAT TAKES TALENT, ESPECIALLY WHEN YOU HAVE NO FEET.

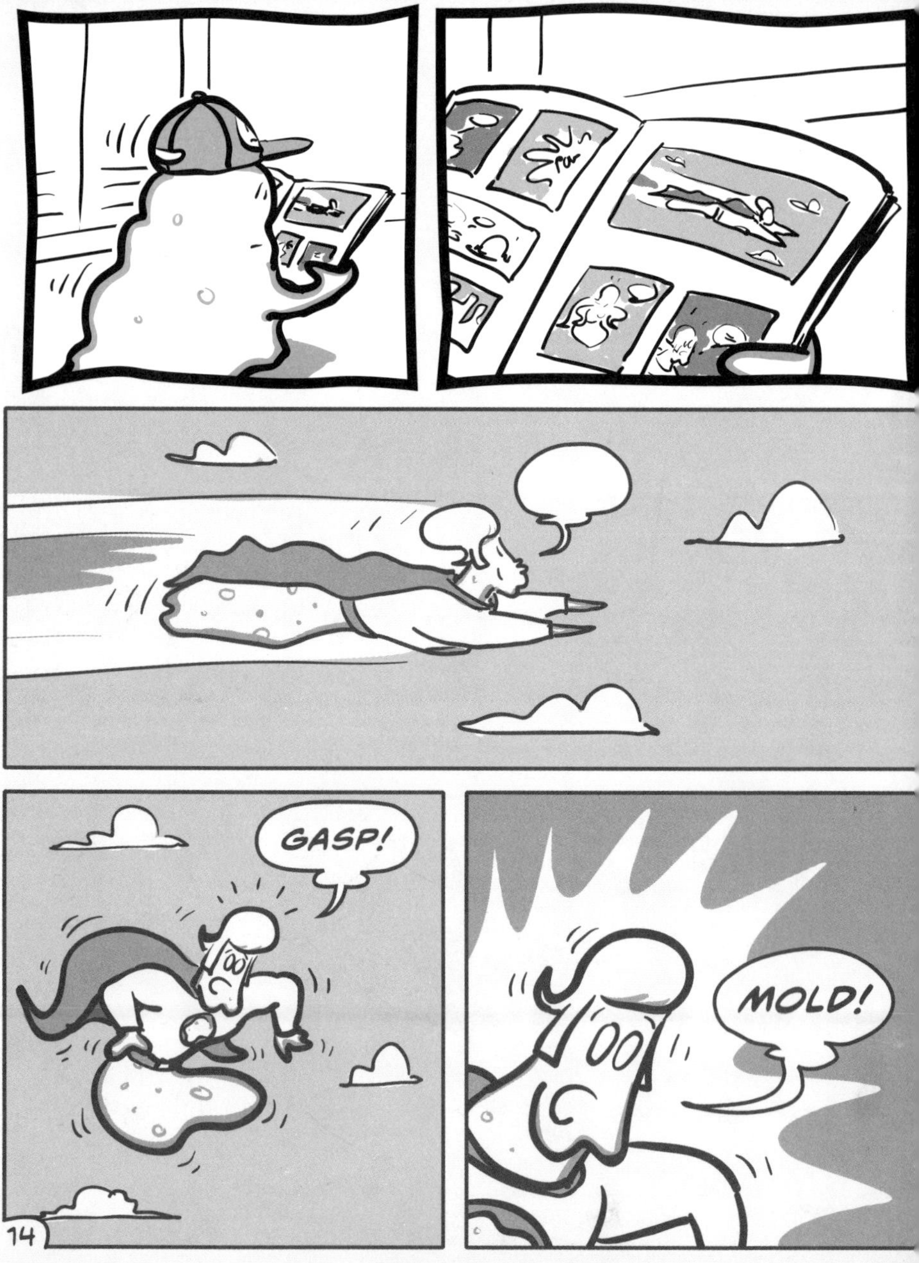
GASP!
MOLD!

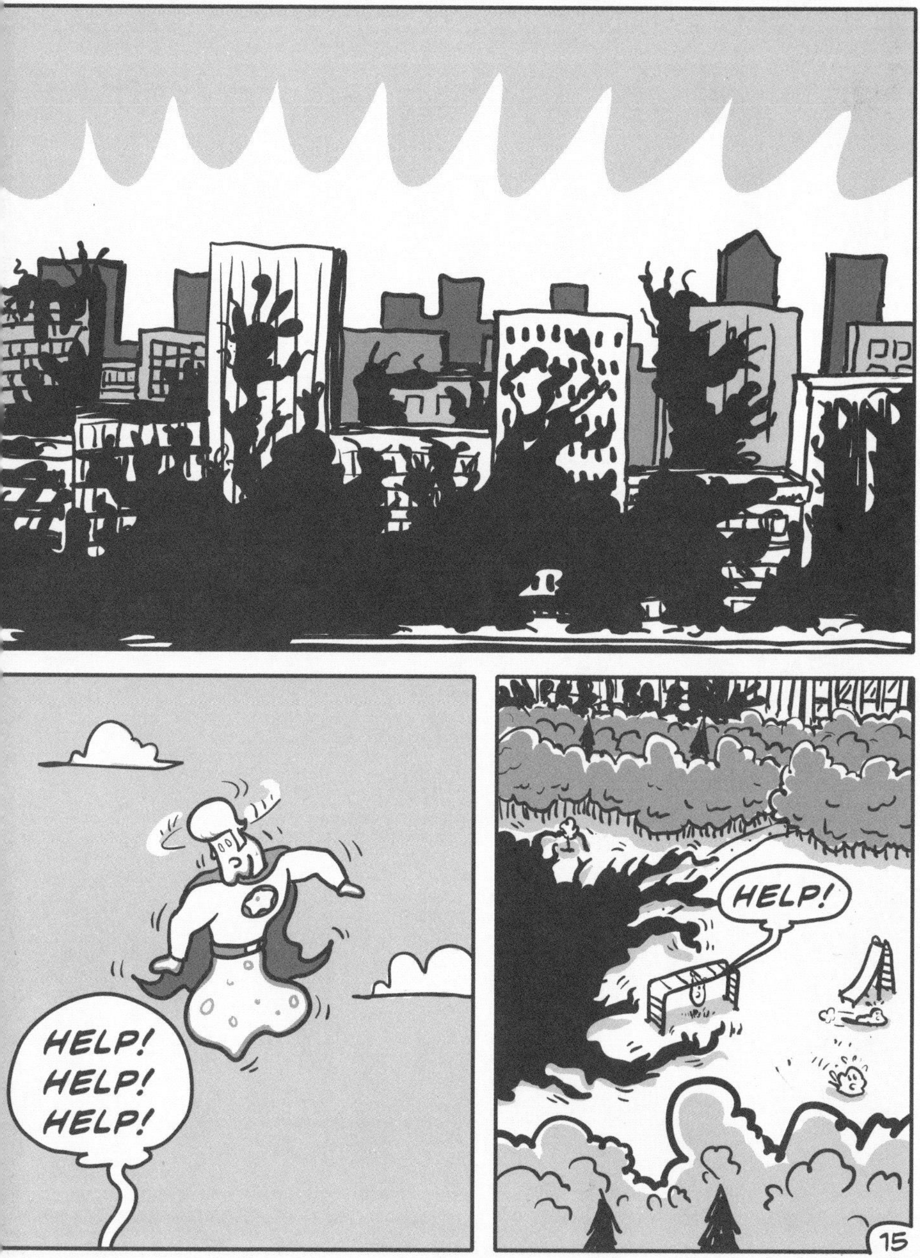
HELP! HELP! HELP!
HELP!

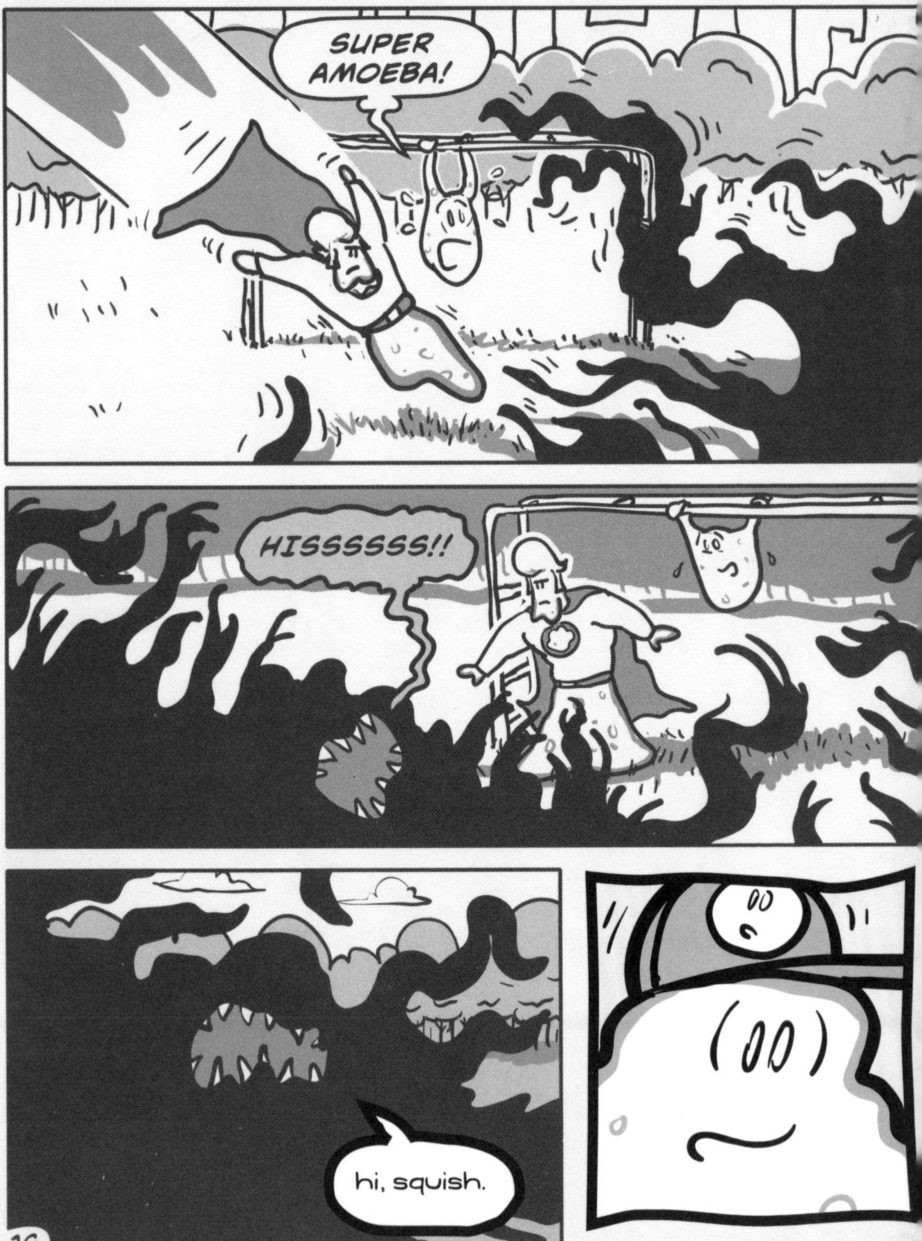
SUPER AMOEBA!
HISSSSSS!!
hi, squish.

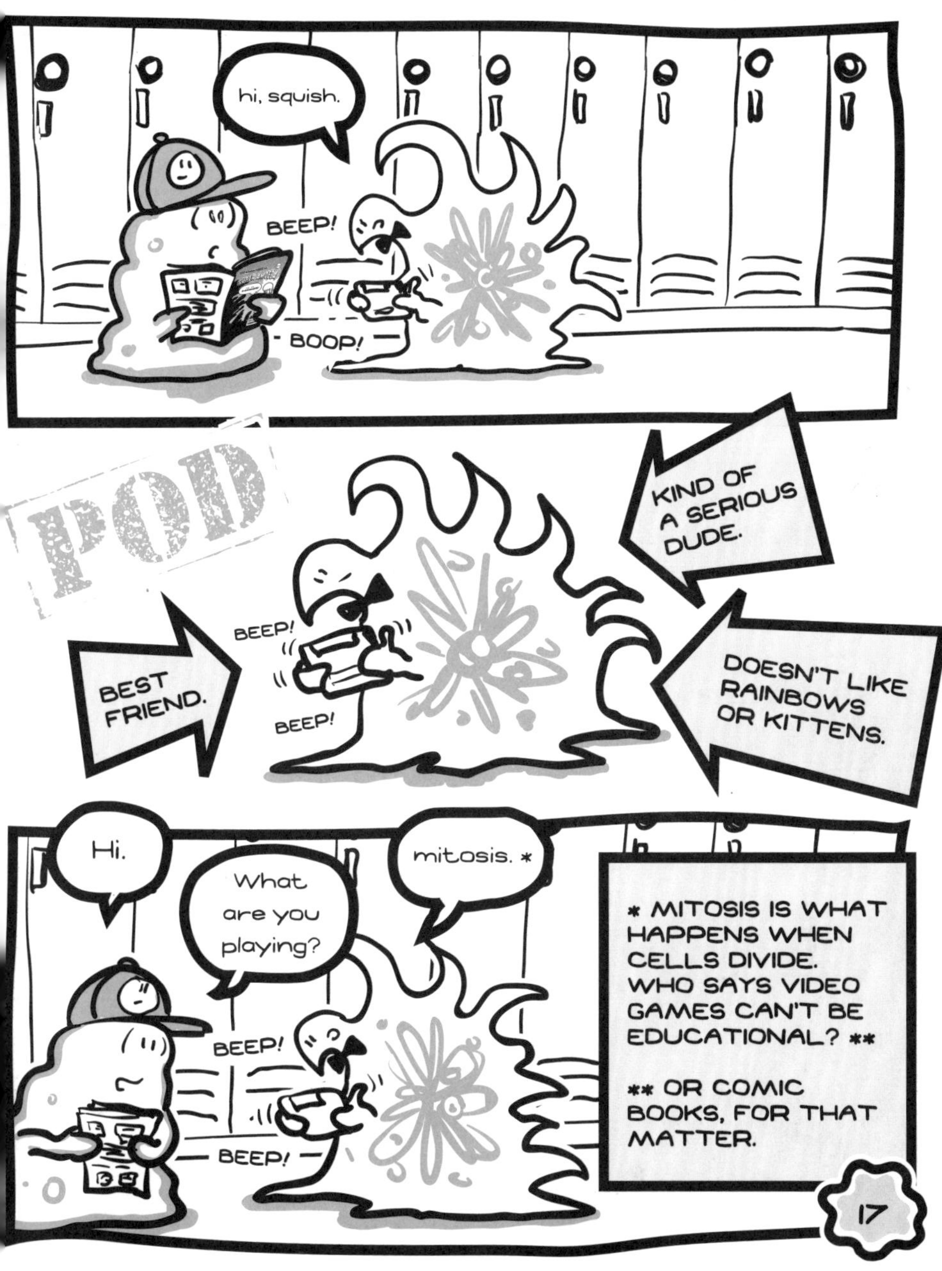

hi, squish.
BEEP!
BOOP!
POD
BEST FRIEND.
BEEP!
BEEP!
KIND OF A SERIOUS DUDE.
DOESN'T LIKE RAINBOWS OR KITTENS.
Hi.
What are you playing?
mitosis. *
BEEP!
BEEP!
* MITOSIS IS WHAT HAPPENS WHEN CELLS DIVIDE. WHO SAYS VIDEO GAMES CAN'T BE EDUCATIONAL? **
** OR COMIC BOOKS, FOR THAT MATTER.

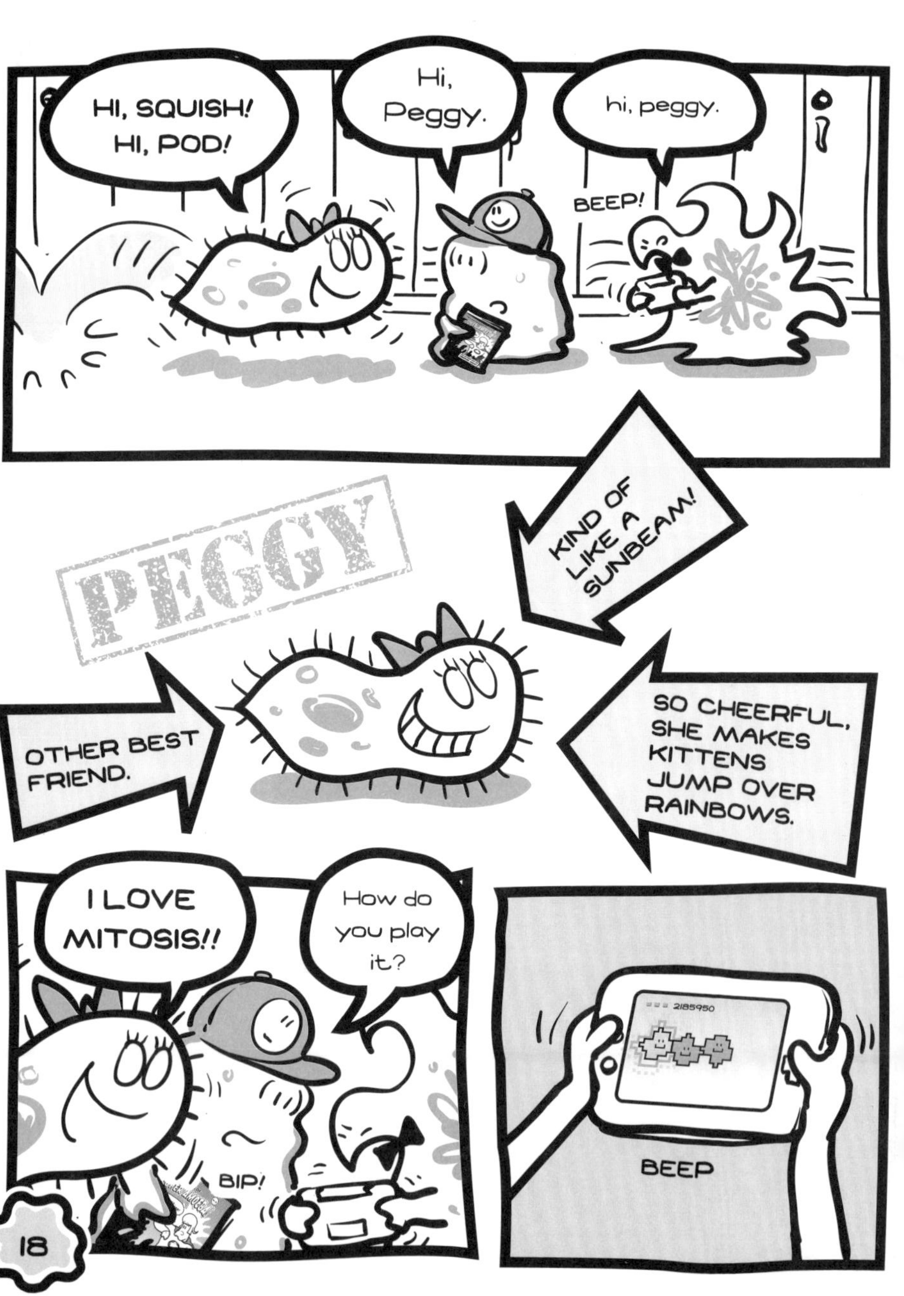

HI, SQUISH! HI, POD!
Hi, Peggy.
hi, peggy.
BEEP!
PEGGY
KIND OF LIKE A SUNBEAM!
OTHER BEST FRIEND.
SO CHEERFUL, SHE MAKES KITTENS JUMP OVER RAINBOWS.
I LOVE MITOSIS!!
How do you play it?
BIP!
2185950
BEEP

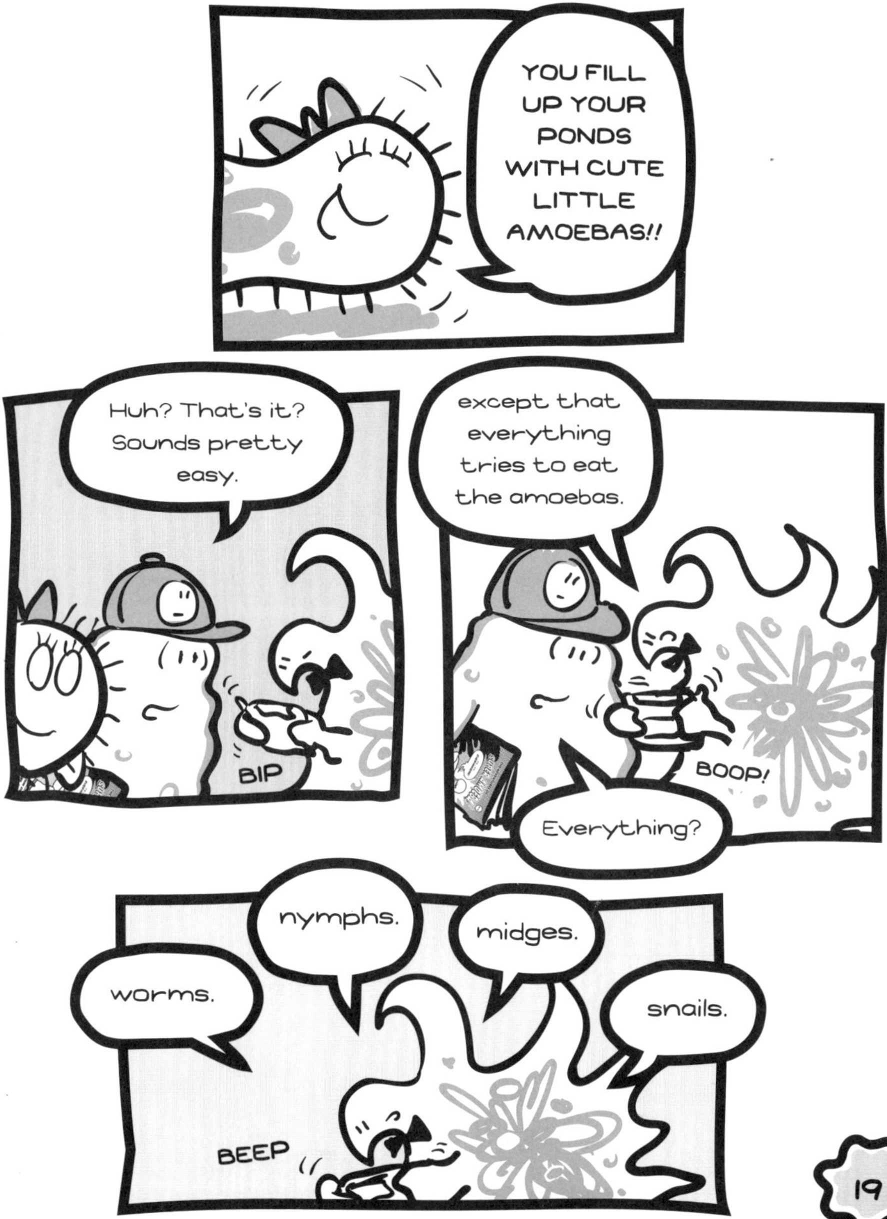
YOU FILL UP YOUR PONDS WITH CUTE LITTLE AMOEBAS!!
Huh? That's it? Sounds pretty easy.
BIP
except that everything tries to eat the amoebas.
BOOP!
Everything?
worms.
nymphs.
midges.
snails.
BEEP

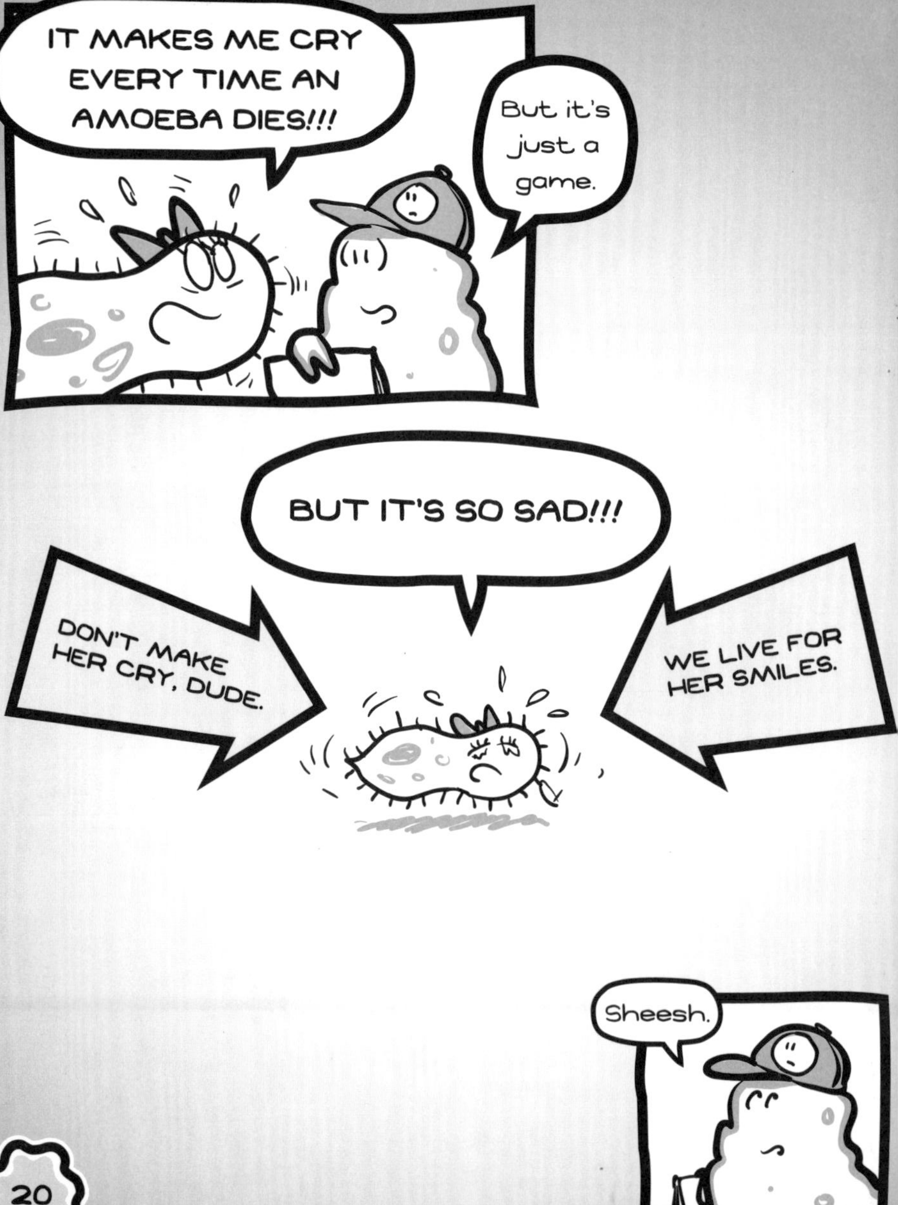

IT MAKES ME CRY EVERY TIME AN AMOEBA DIES!!!
But it's just a game.
BUT IT'S SO SAD!!!
DON'T MAKE HER CRY, DUDE.
WE LIVE FOR HER SMILES.
Sheesh.

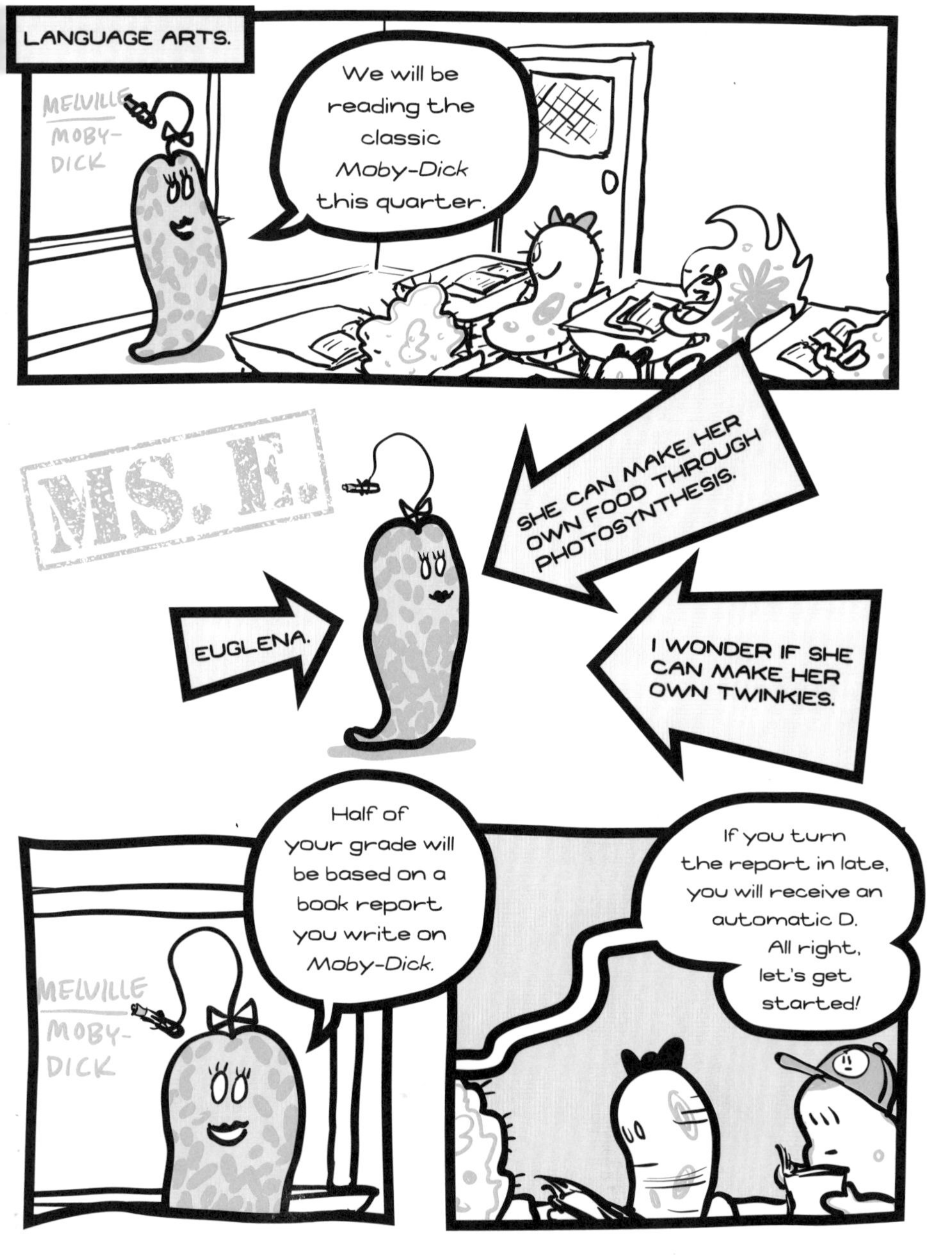

LANGUAGE ARTS.
MELVILLE
MOBY-DICK
We will be reading the classic *Moby-Dick* this quarter.
MS. E.
EUGLENA.
SHE CAN MAKE HER OWN FOOD THROUGH PHOTOSYNTHESIS.
I WONDER IF SHE CAN MAKE HER OWN TWINKIES.
MELVILLE
MOBY-DICK
Half of your grade will be based on a book report you write on *Moby-Dick*.
If you turn the report in late, you will receive an automatic D. All right, let's get started!

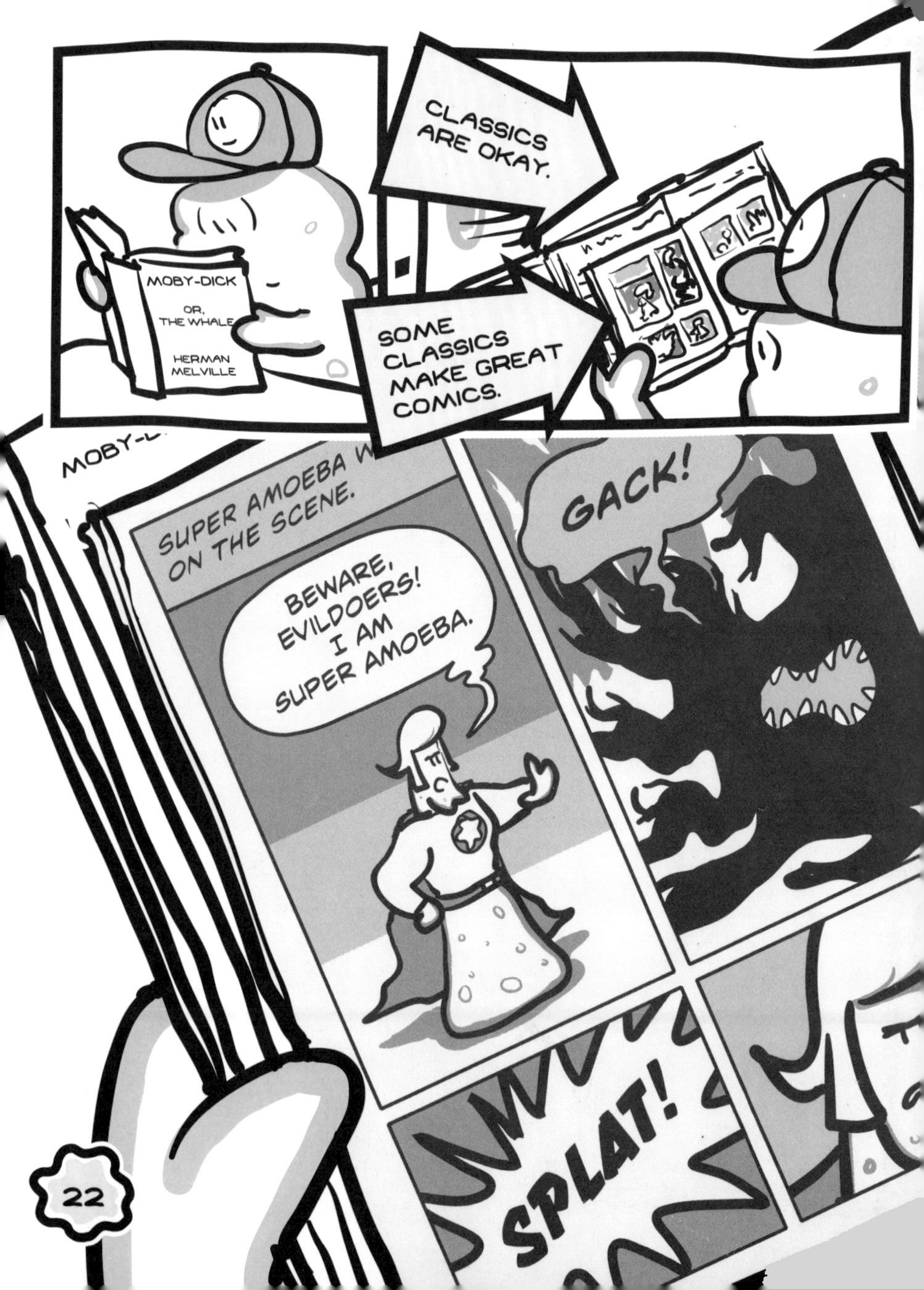

MOBY-DICK
OR, THE WHALE
HERMAN MELVILLE
CLASSICS ARE OKAY.
SOME CLASSICS MAKE GREAT COMICS.
SUPER AMOEBA W
ON THE SCENE.
BEWARE, EVILDOERS! I AM SUPER AMOEBA.
GACK!
SPLAT!

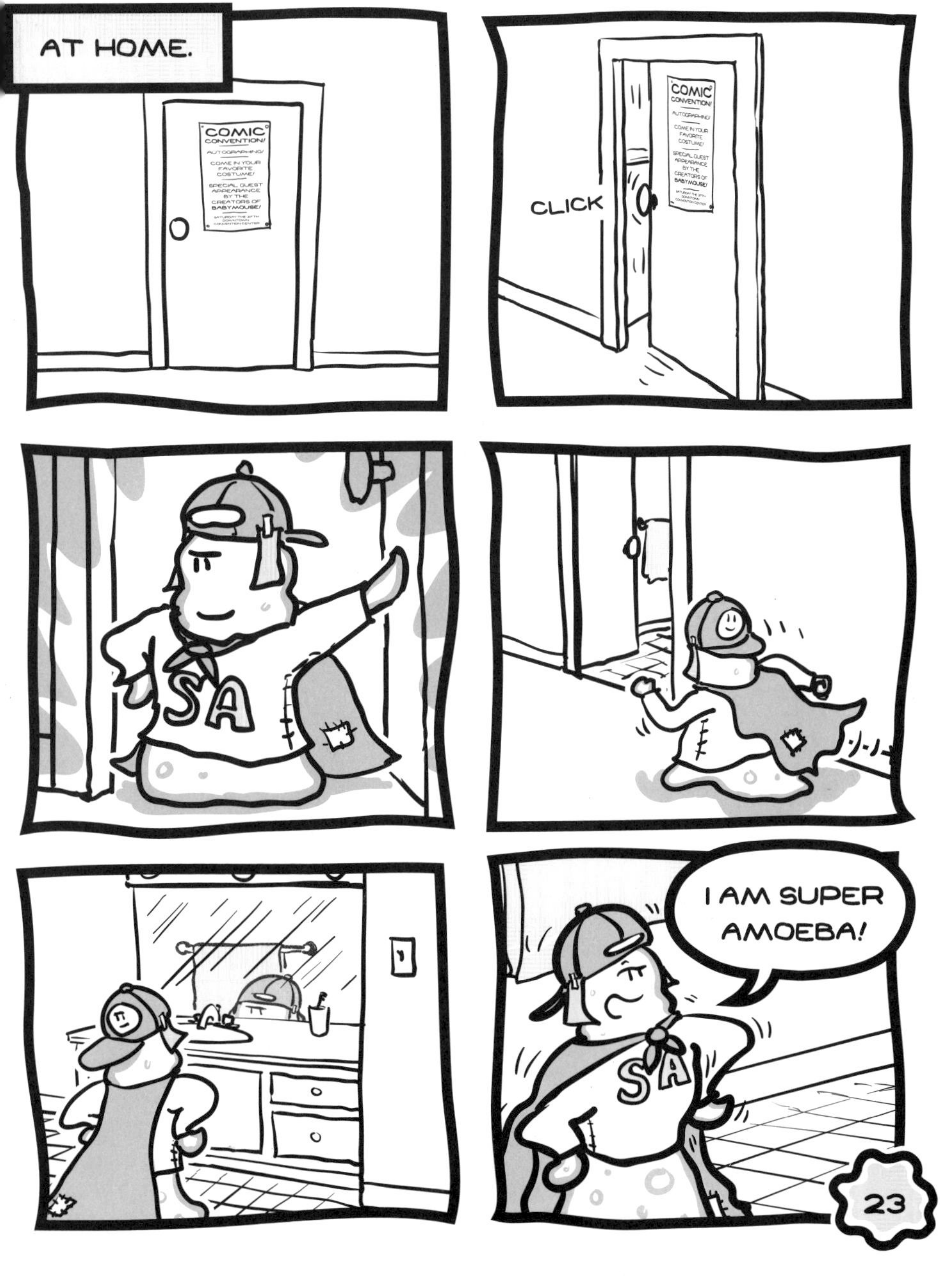
AT HOME.
COMIC CONVENTION!
AUTOGRAPHING!
COME IN YOUR FAVORITE COSTUME!
SPECIAL GUEST APPEARANCE BY THE CREATORS OF BABYMOUSE!
CLICK
I AM SUPER AMOEBA!

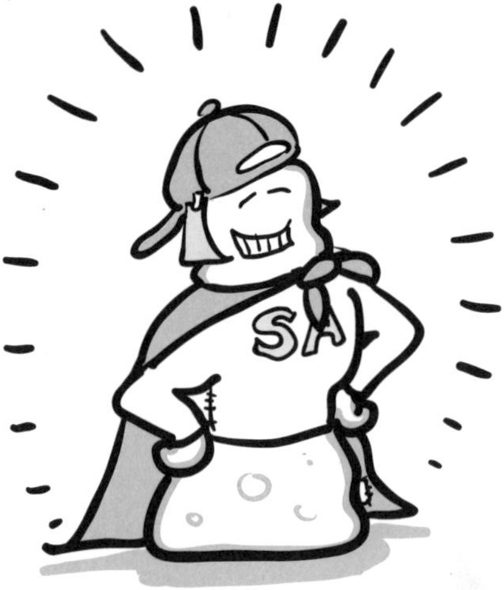

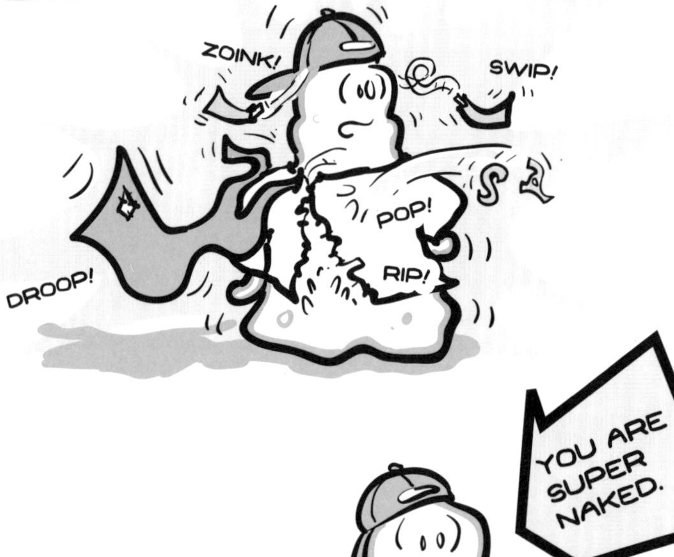
ZOINK!
SWIP!
POP!
RIP!
DROOP!

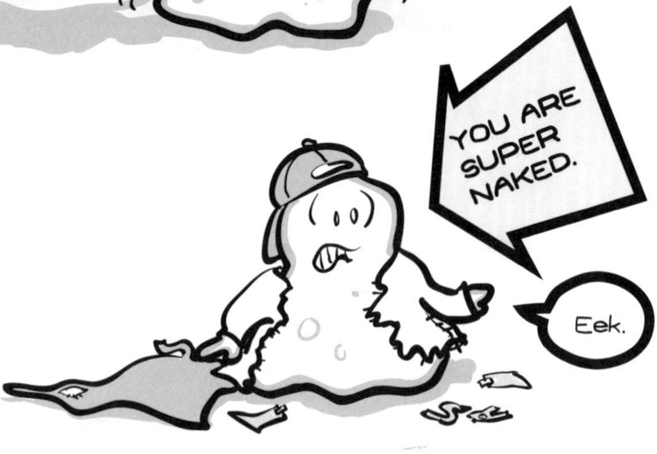
YOU ARE SUPER NAKED.
Eek.

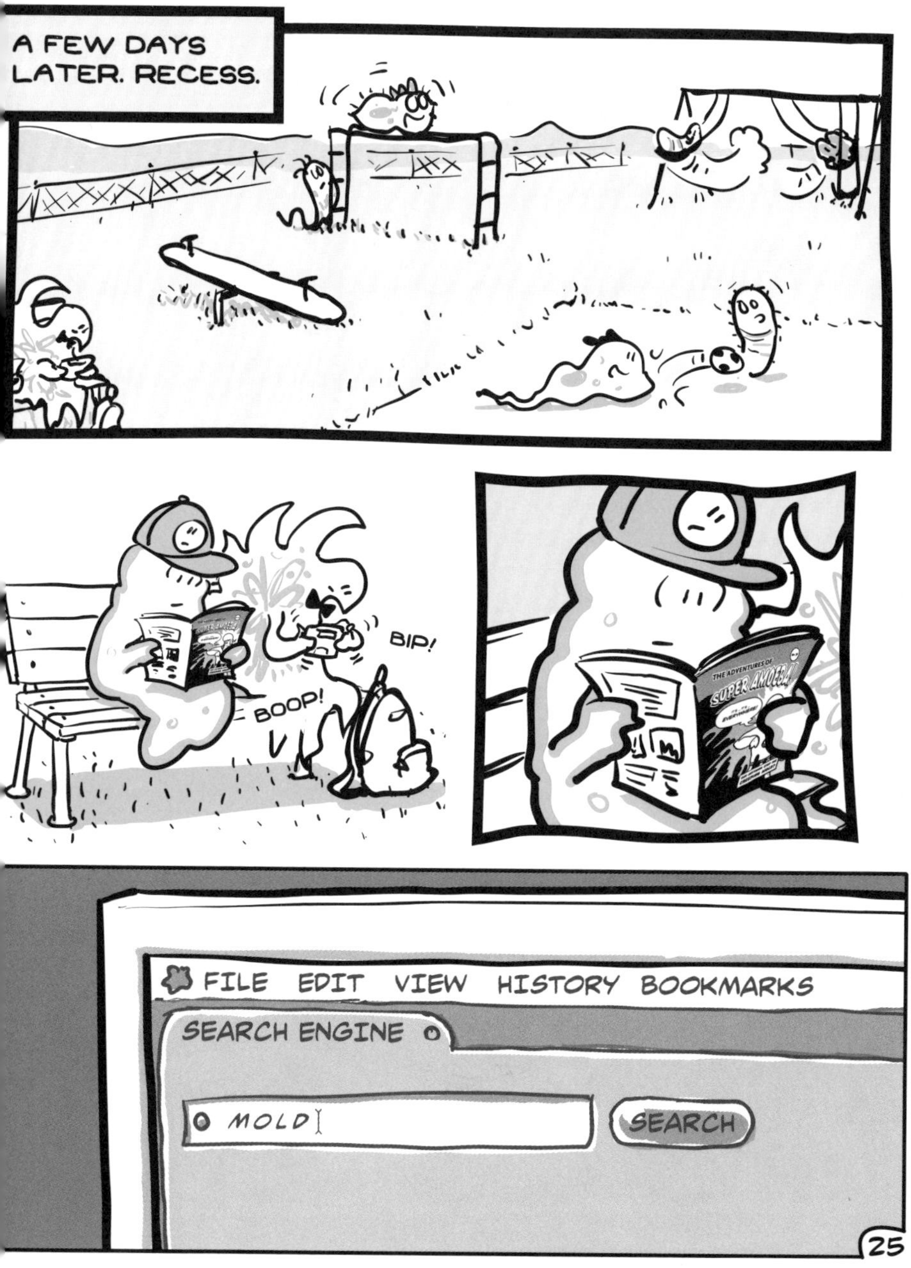
A FEW DAYS LATER. RECESS.
BIP!
BOOP!
THE ADVENTURES OF SUPER AMOEBA!
FILE EDIT VIEW HISTORY BOOKMARKS
SEARCH ENGINE
MOLD
SEARCH

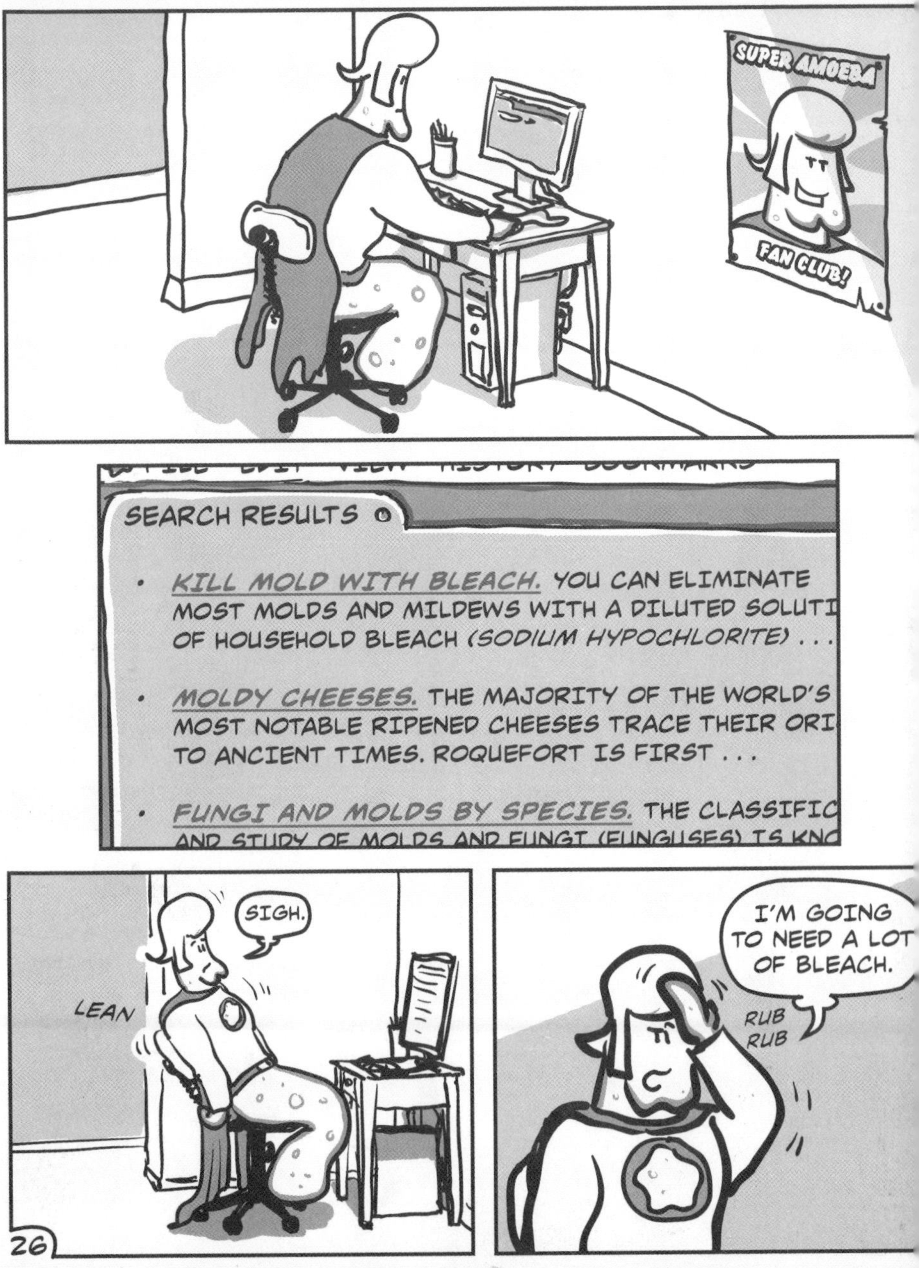
SUPER AMOEBA
FAN CLUB!
SEARCH RESULTS
• KILL MOLD WITH BLEACH. YOU CAN ELIMINATE MOST MOLDS AND MILDEWS WITH A DILUTED SOLUTI OF HOUSEHOLD BLEACH (SODIUM HYPOCHLORITE) . . .
• MOLDY CHEESES. THE MAJORITY OF THE WORLD'S MOST NOTABLE RIPENED CHEESES TRACE THEIR ORI TO ANCIENT TIMES. ROQUEFORT IS FIRST . . .
• FUNGI AND MOLDS BY SPECIES. THE CLASSIFIC
SIGH.
LEAN
I'M GOING TO NEED A LOT OF BLEACH.
RUB RUB

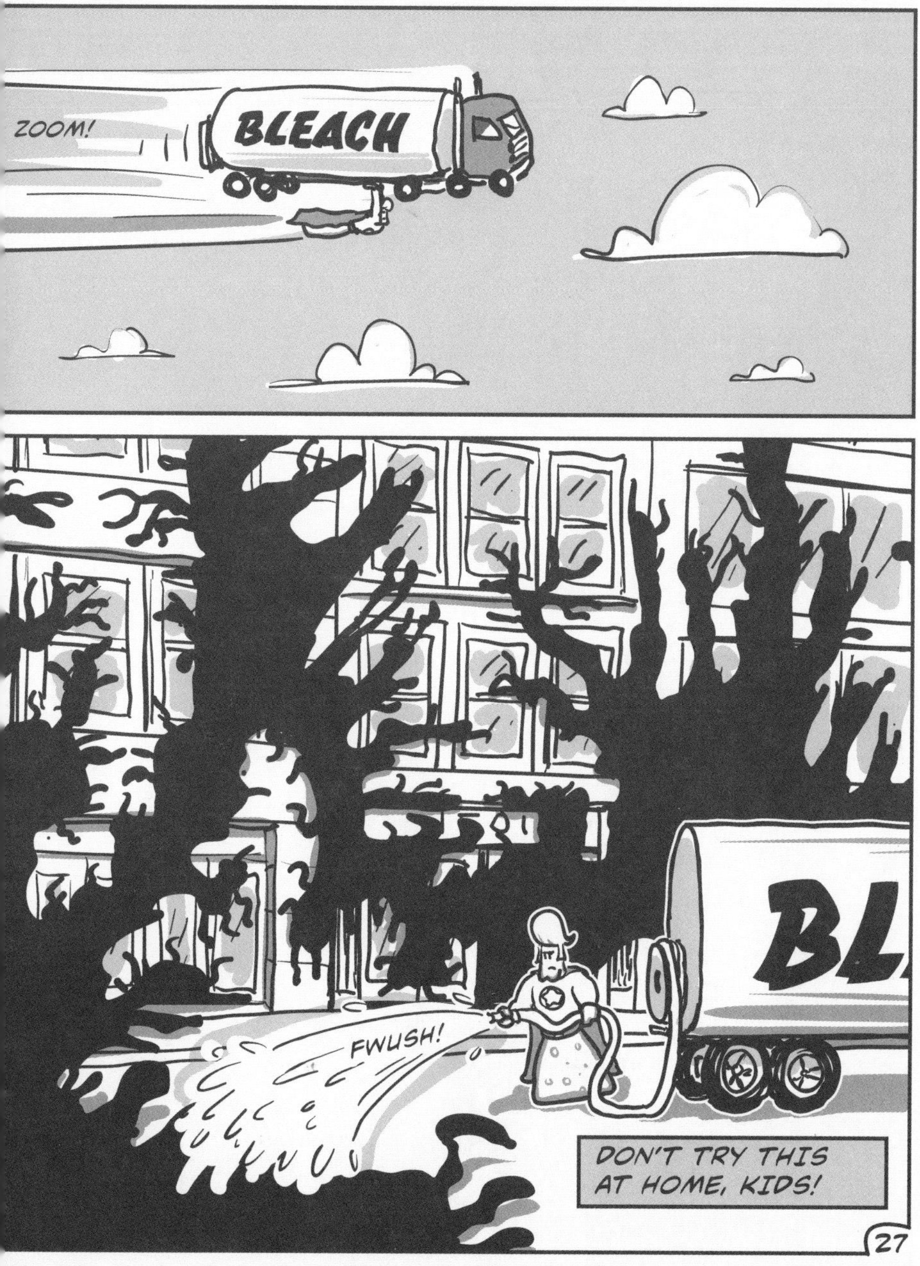
ZOOM!
BLEACH
FWUSH!
BL
DON'T TRY THIS AT HOME, KIDS!

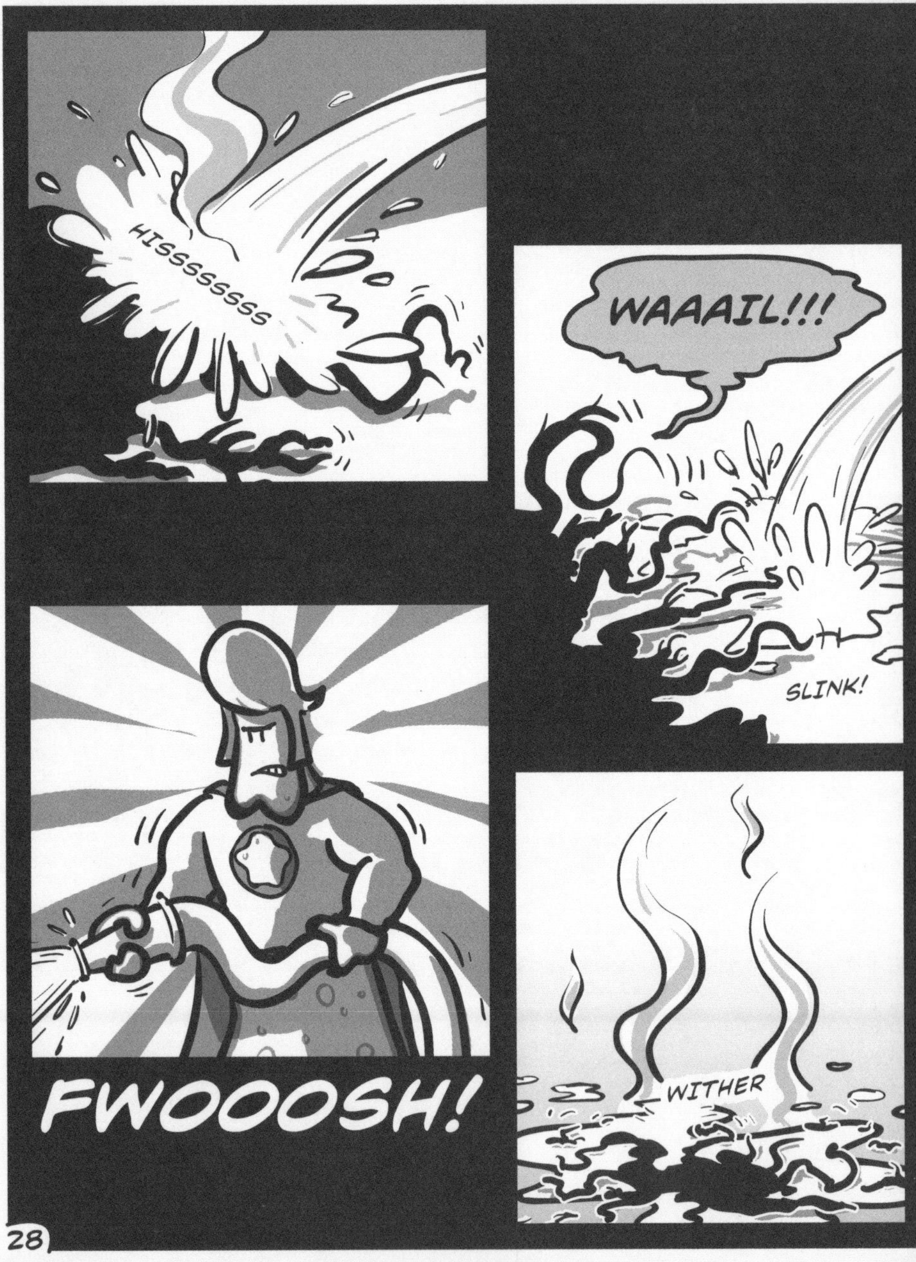
HISSSSSSSSS
WAAAIL!!!
SLINK!
FWOOOSH!
WITHER

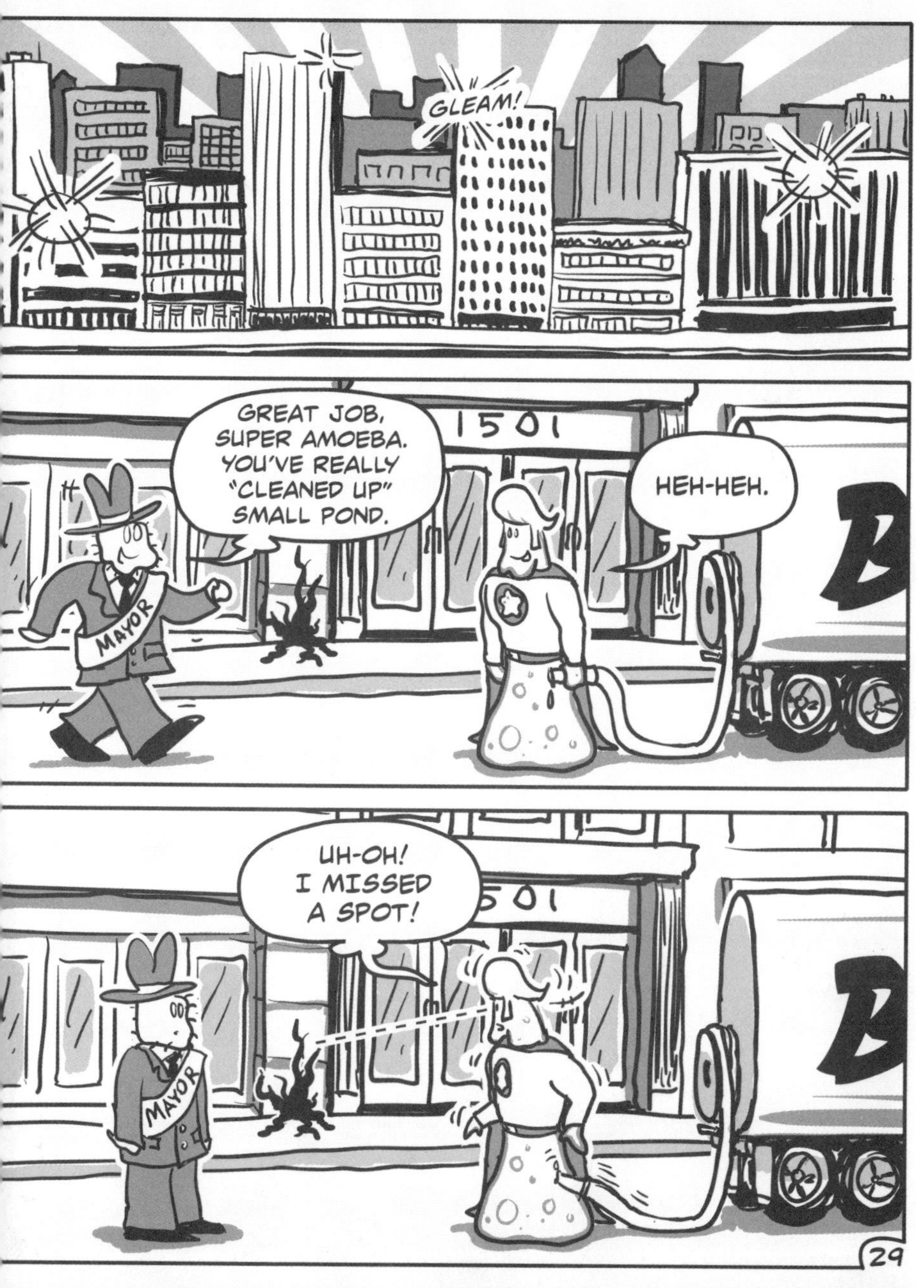
GLEAM!
GREAT JOB, SUPER AMOEBA. YOU'VE REALLY "CLEANED UP" SMALL POND.
HEH-HEH.
MAYOR
UH-OH! I MISSED A SPOT!

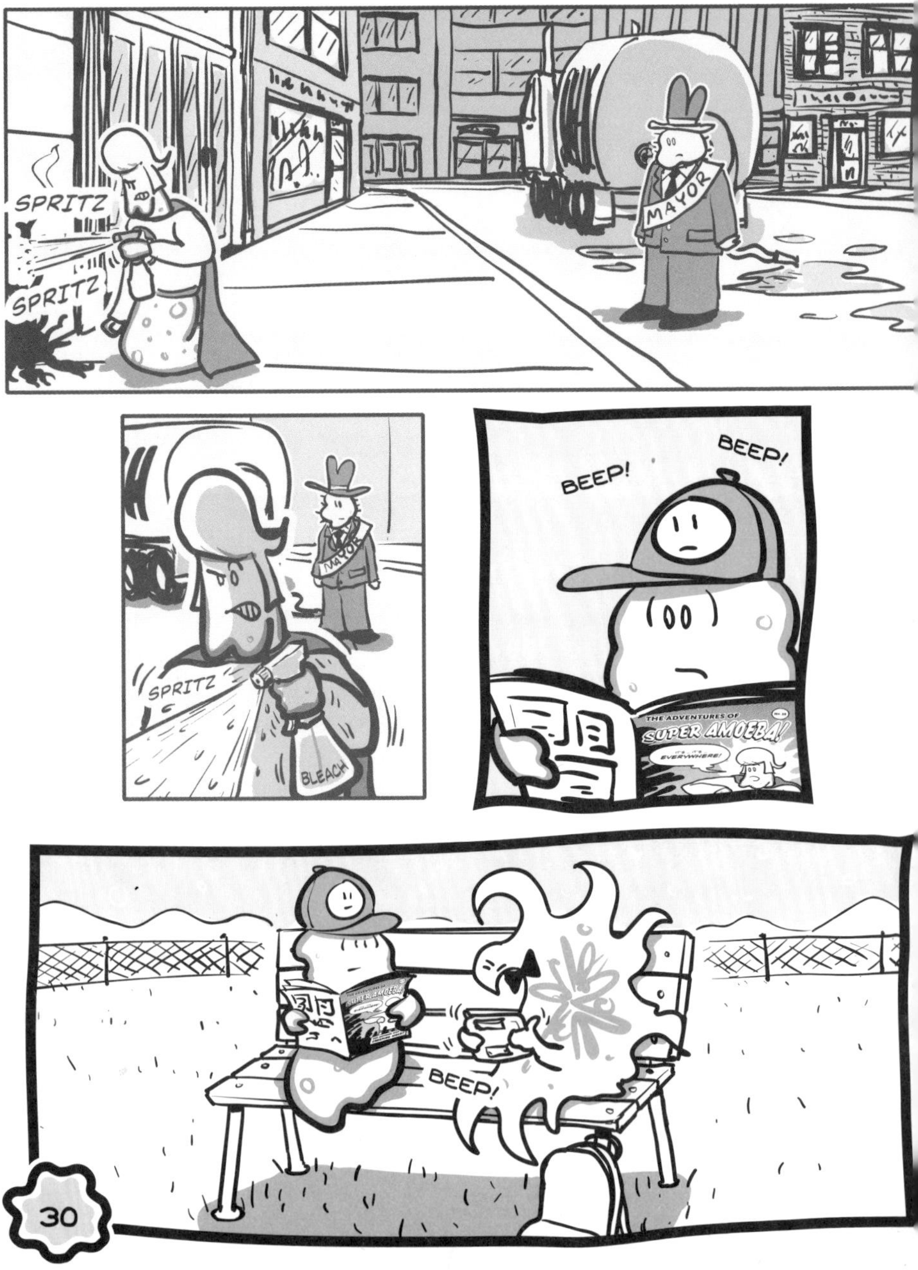
SPRITZ
SPRITZ
MAYOR
SPRITZ
MAYOR
BLEACH
BEEP!
BEEP!
THE ADVENTURES OF
SUPER AMOEBA!
IT'S... IT'S EVERYWHERE!
BEEP!

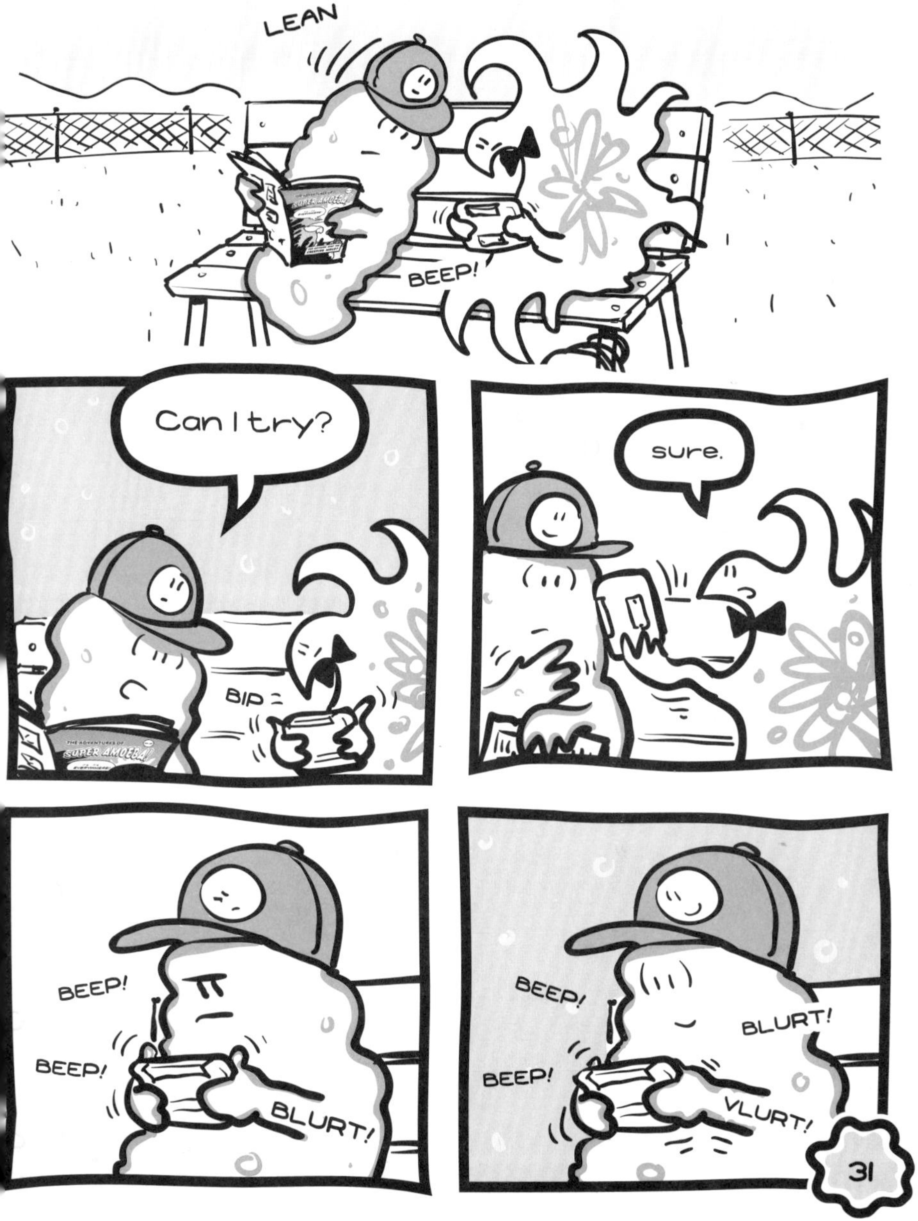
LEAN
BEEP!
Can I try?
BIP
sure.
BEEP!
BEEP!
BLURT!
BEEP!
BEEP!
BLURT!
VLURT!

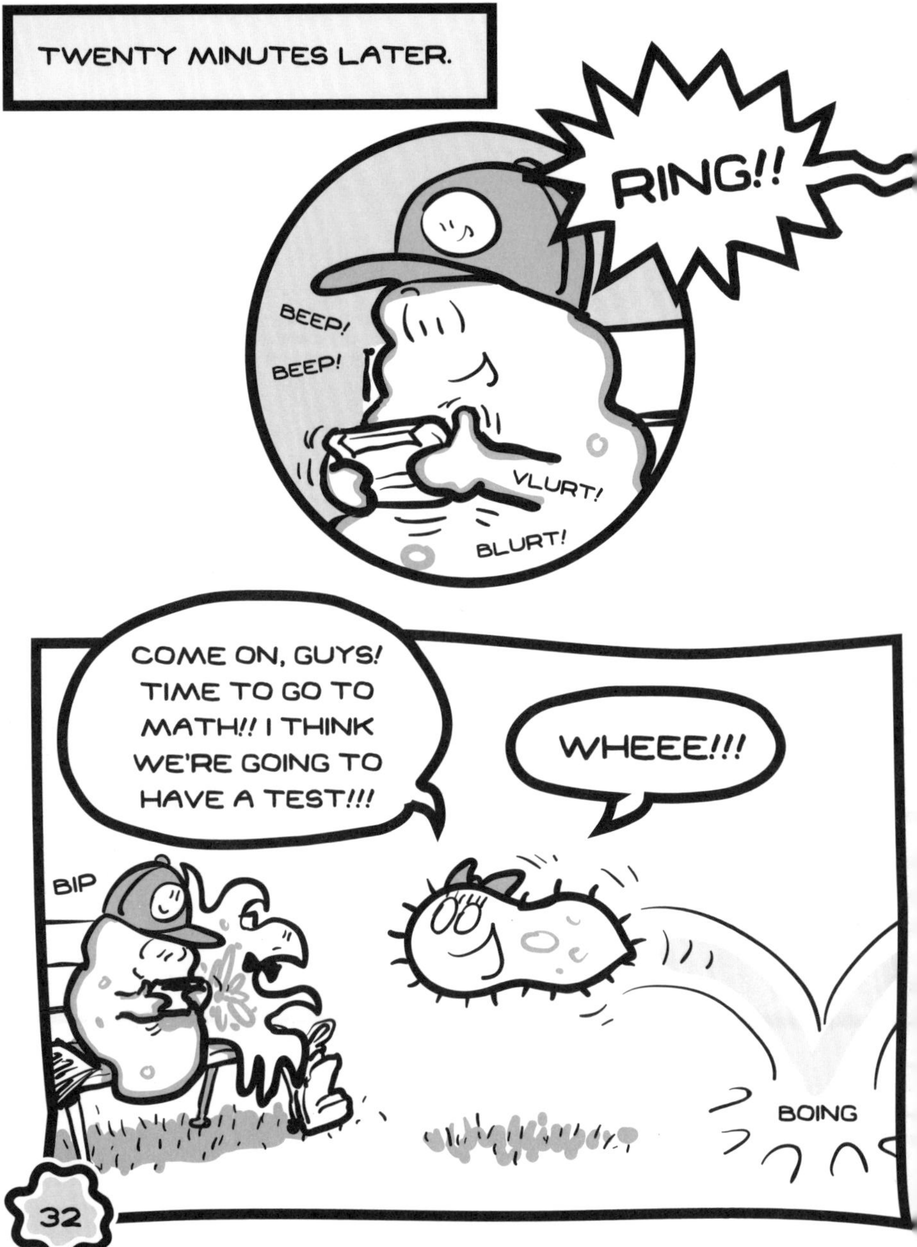
TWENTY MINUTES LATER.
RING!!
BEEP!
BEEP!
VLURT!
BLURT!
COME ON, GUYS! TIME TO GO TO MATH!! I THINK WE'RE GOING TO HAVE A TEST!!!
WHEEE!!!
BIP
BOING

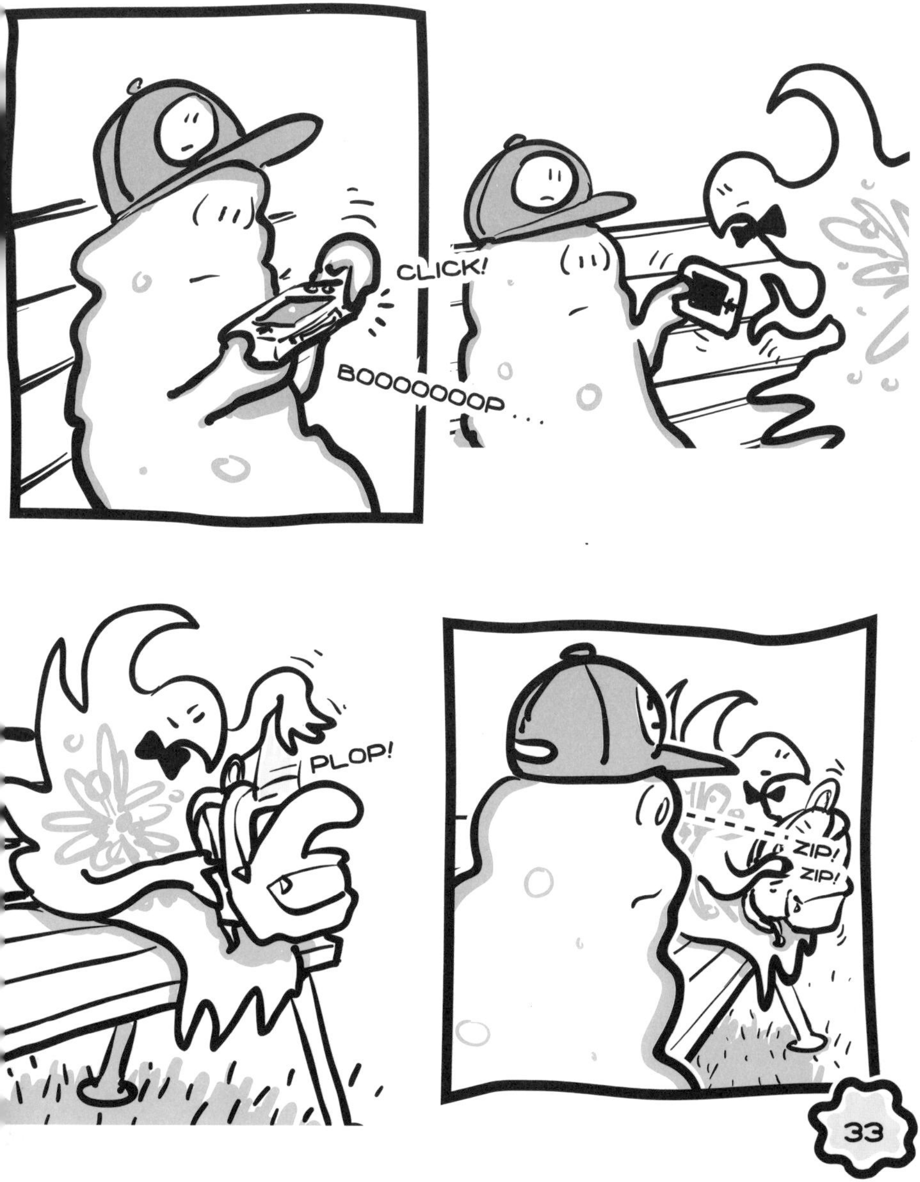
CLICK!
BOOOOOOOP...
PLOP!
ZIP!
ZIP!

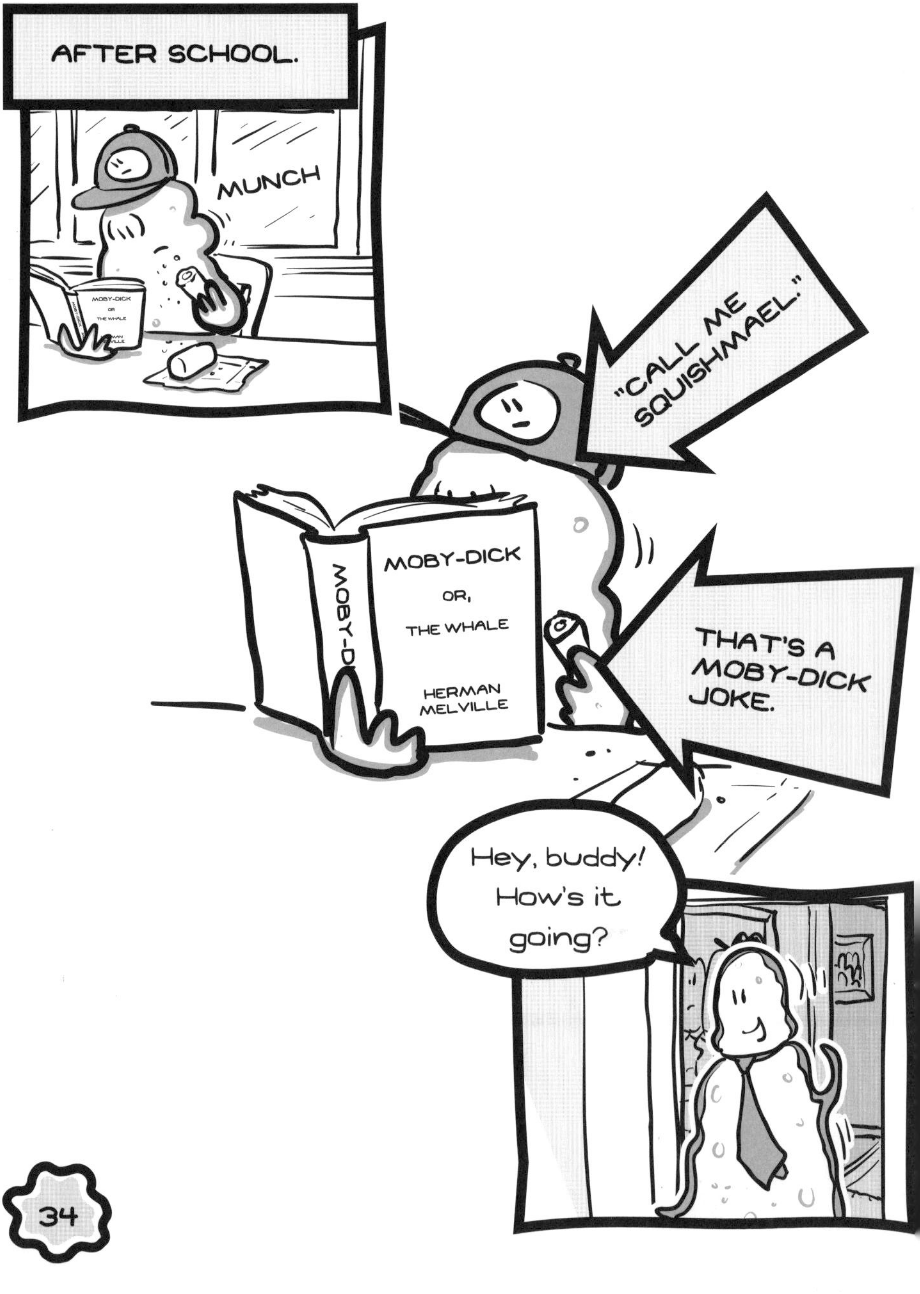
AFTER SCHOOL.
MUNCH
MOBY-DICK OR, THE WHALE
HERMAN MELVILLE
"CALL ME SQUISHMAEL."
MOBY-DICK
OR,
THE WHALE
HERMAN
MELVILLE
THAT'S A MOBY-DICK JOKE.
Hey, buddy! How's it going?

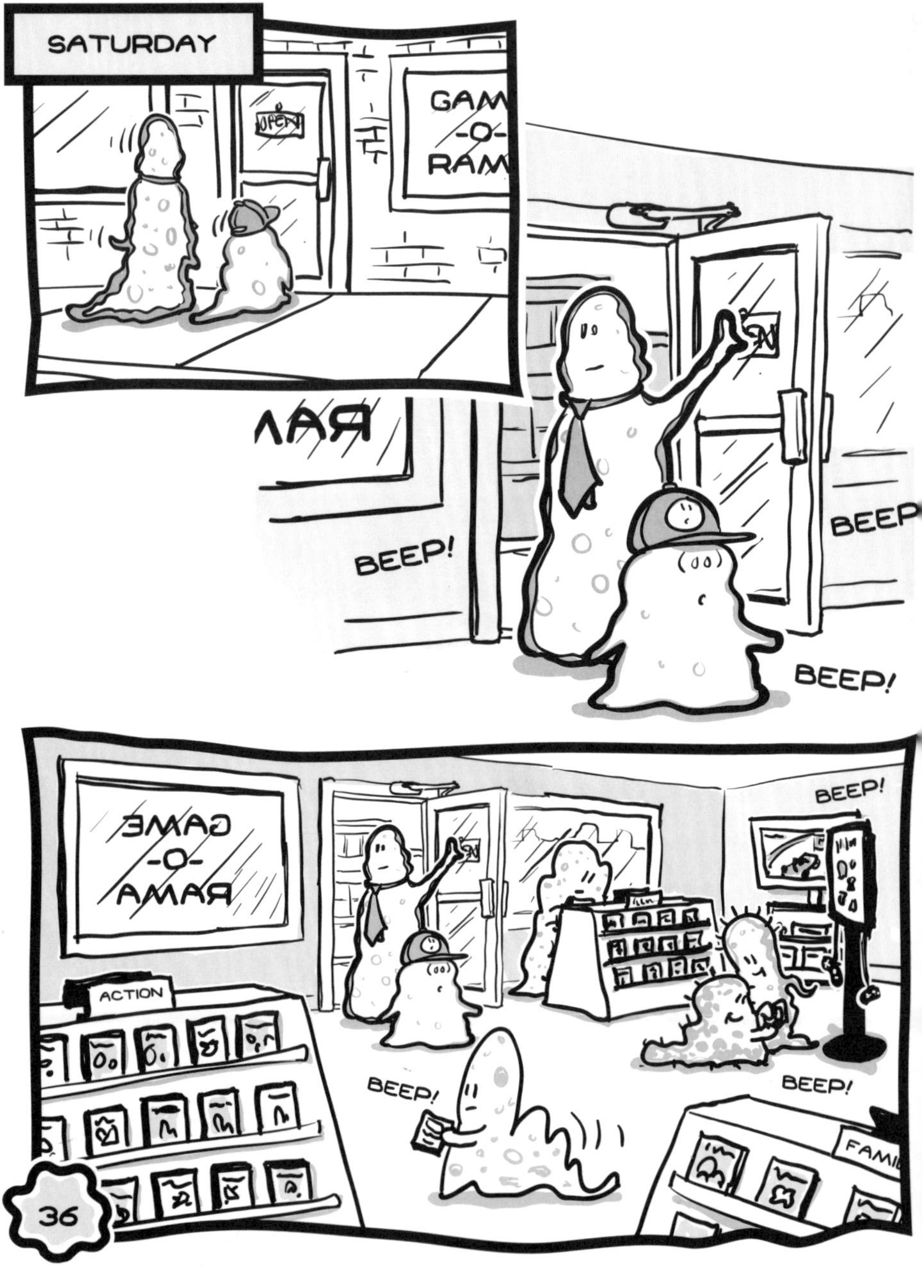
SATURDAY
OPEN
BEEP!
BEEP
BEEP!
BEEP!
ACTION
BEEP!
BEEP!

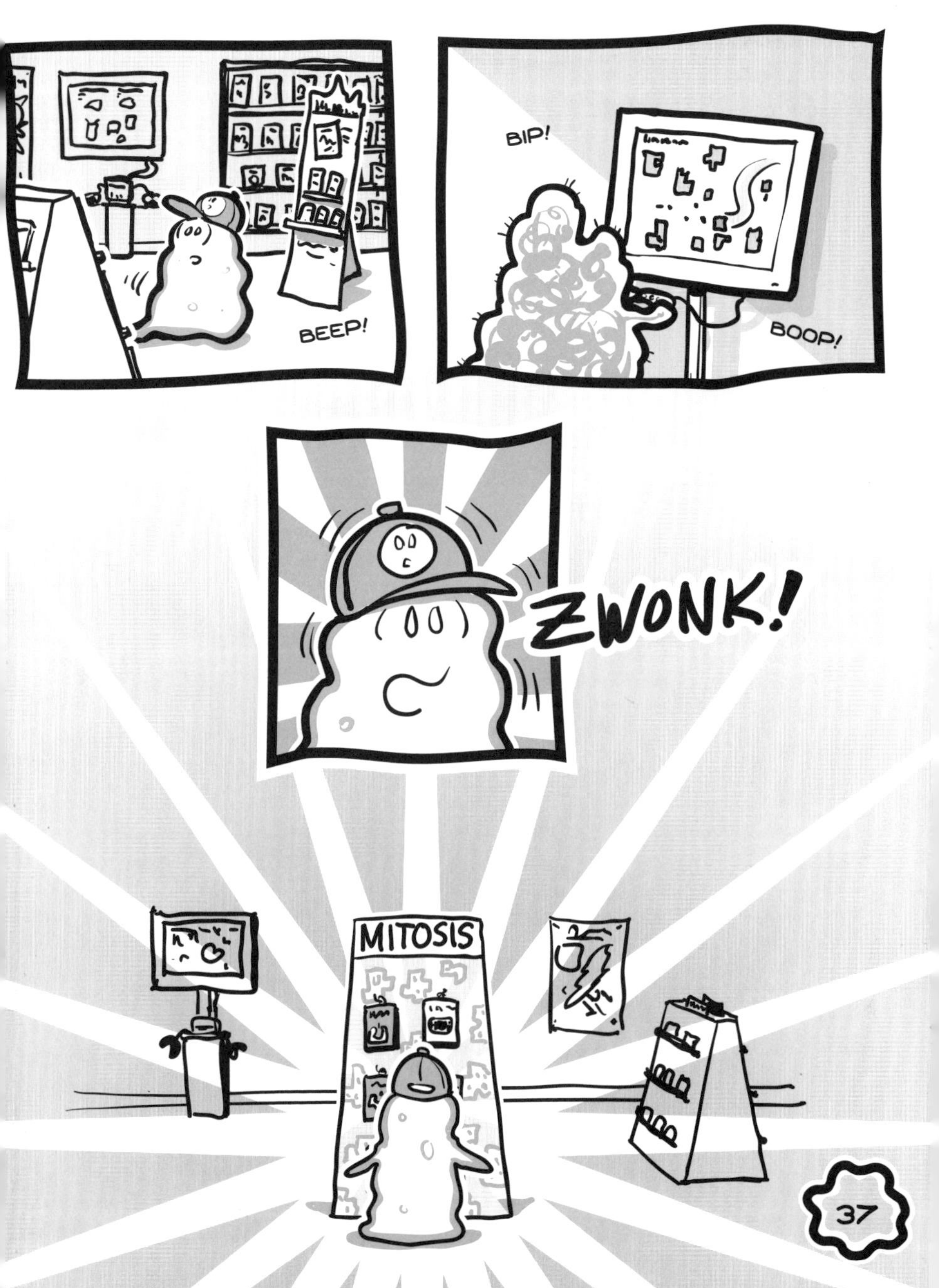
BEEP!
BIP!
BOOP!
ZWONK!
MITOSIS

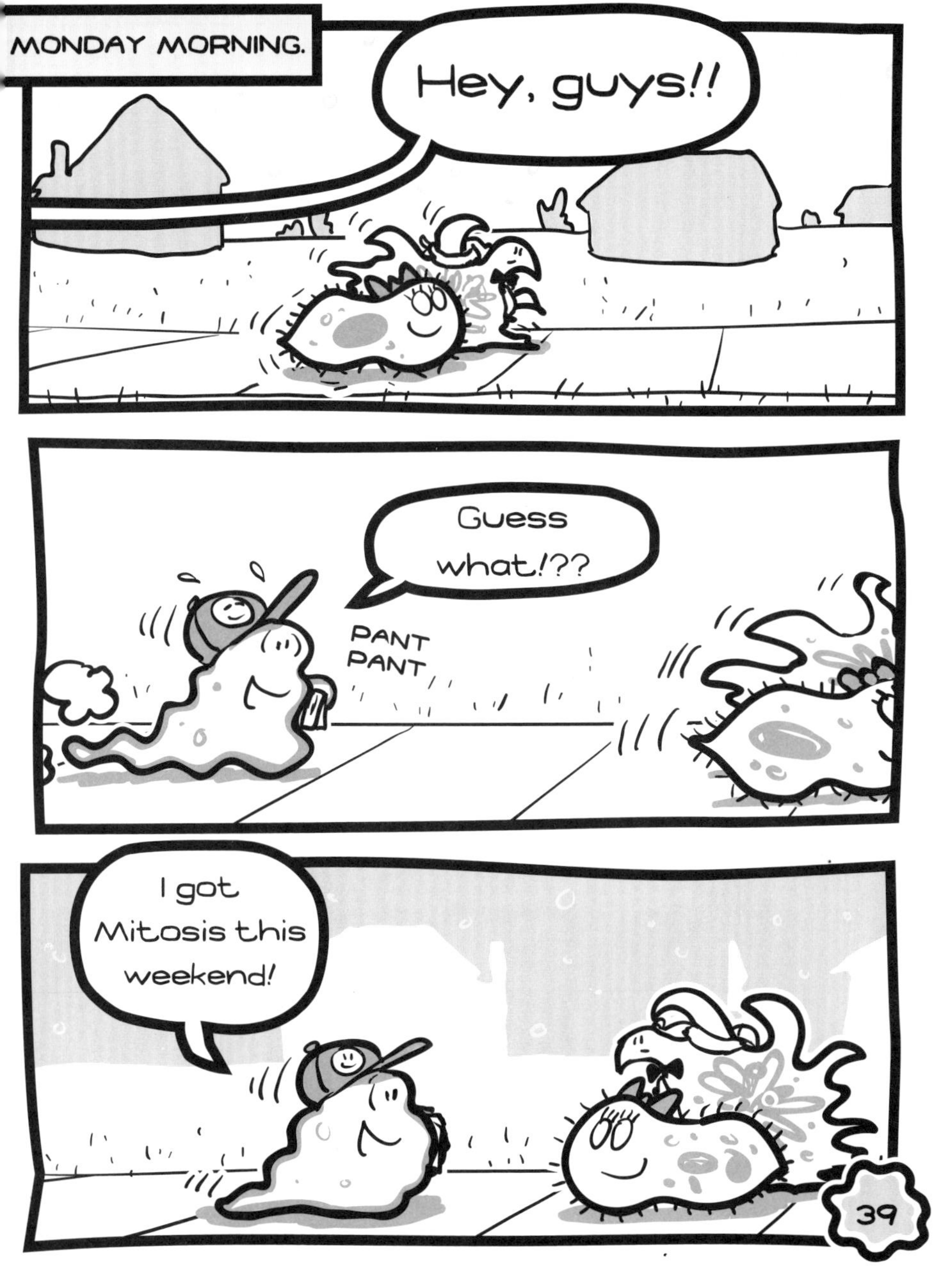
MONDAY MORNING.
Hey, guys!!
Guess what!??
PANT PANT
I got Mitosis this weekend!

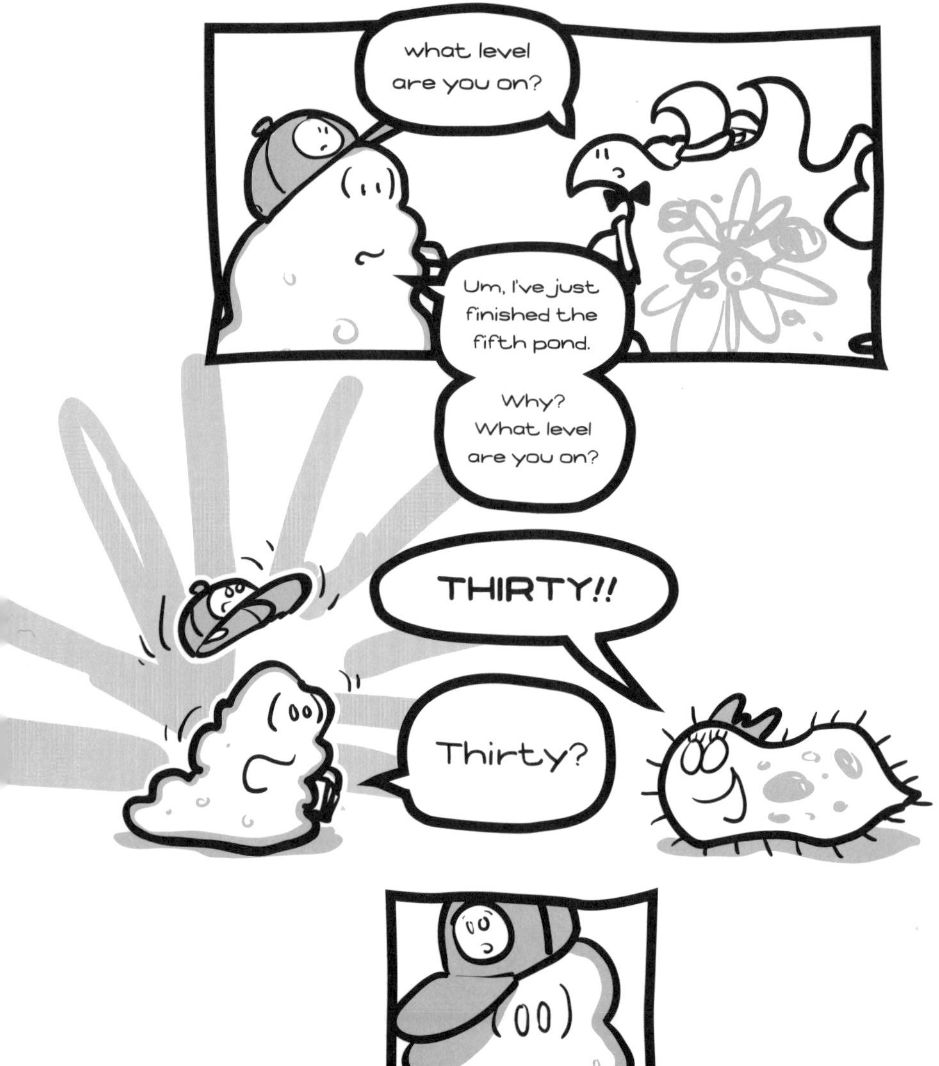
what level are you on?
Um, I've just finished the fifth pond.
Why? What level are you on?
THIRTY!!
Thirty?

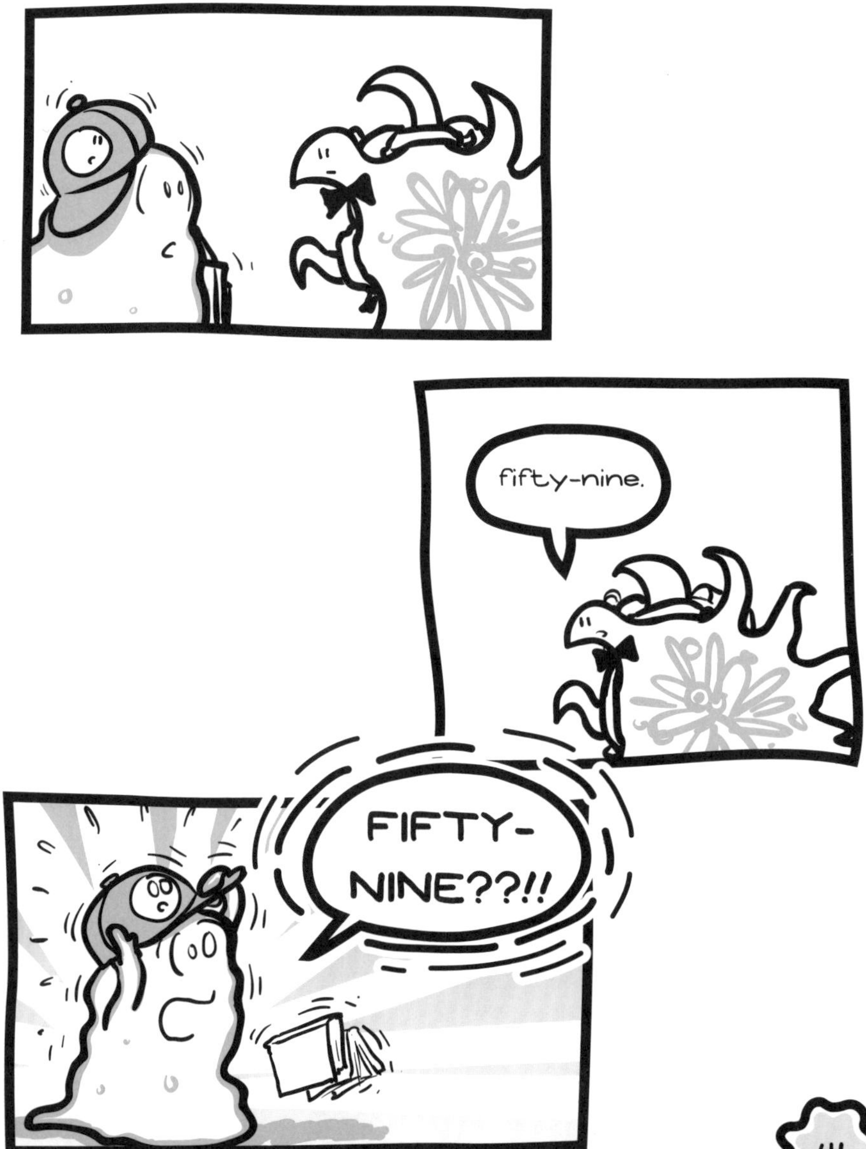
fifty-nine.
FIFTY-NINE??!!

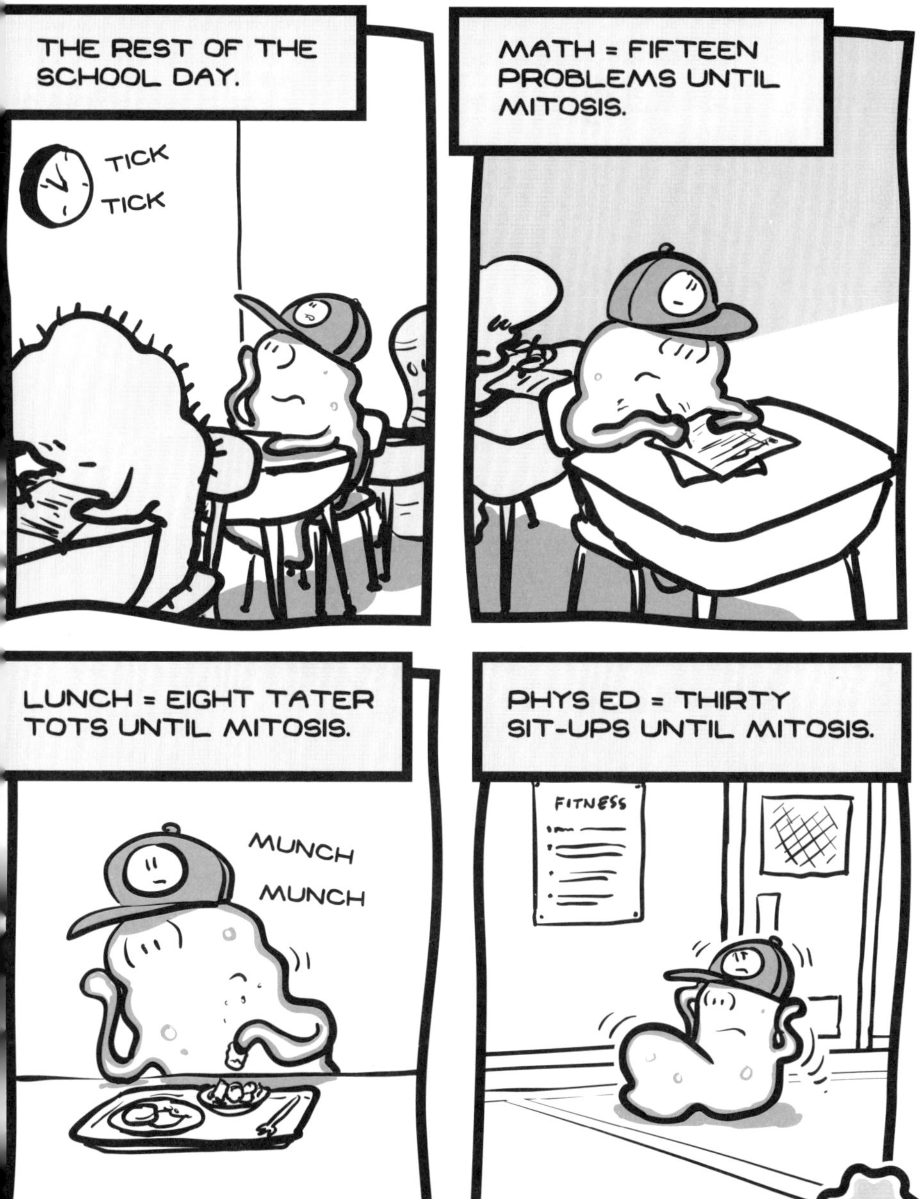
THE REST OF THE SCHOOL DAY.
TICK
TICK
MATH = FIFTEEN PROBLEMS UNTIL MITOSIS.
LUNCH = EIGHT TATER TOTS UNTIL MITOSIS.
MUNCH
MUNCH
PHYS ED = THIRTY SIT-UPS UNTIL MITOSIS.
FITNESS

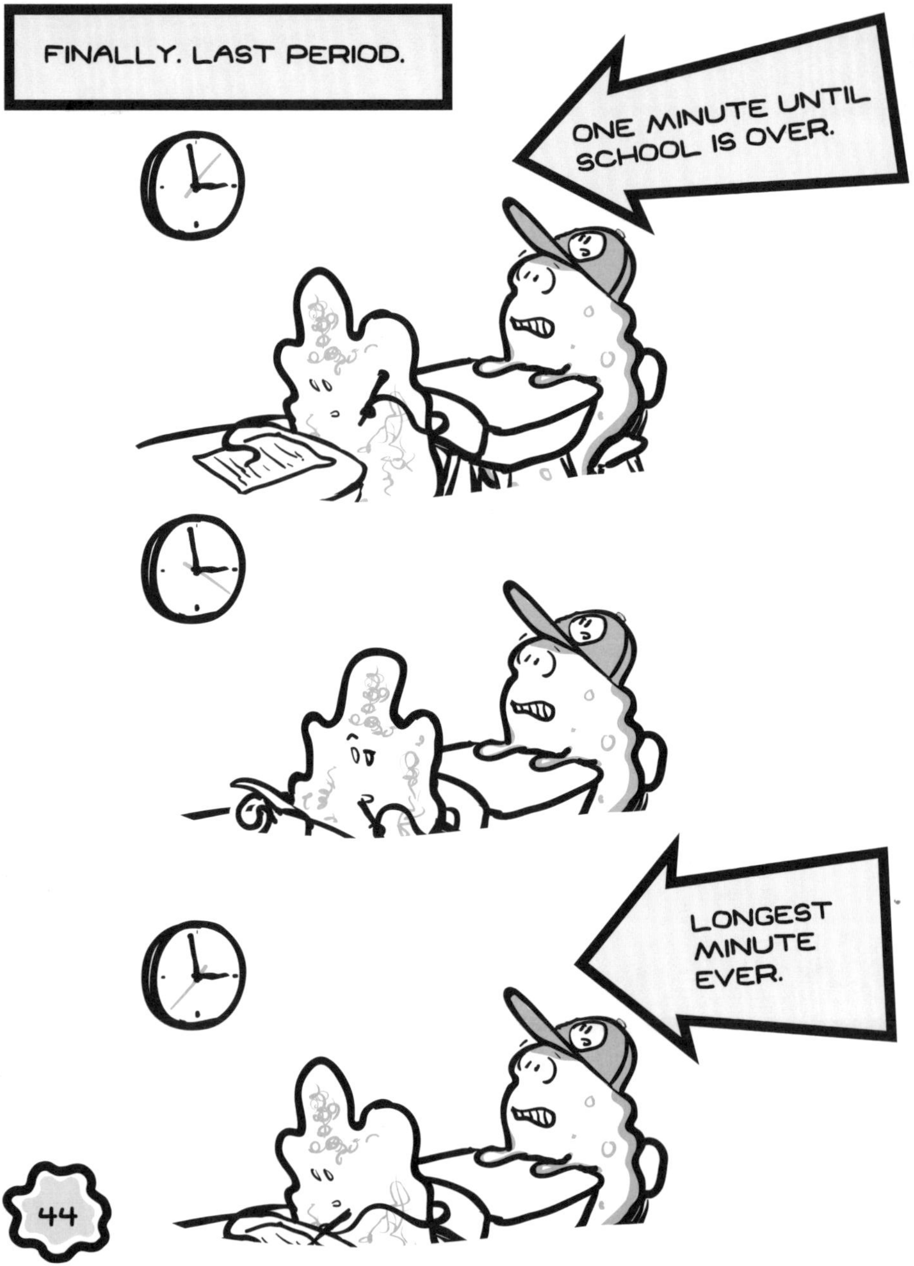
FINALLY. LAST PERIOD.
ONE MINUTE UNTIL SCHOOL IS OVER.
LONGEST MINUTE EVER.

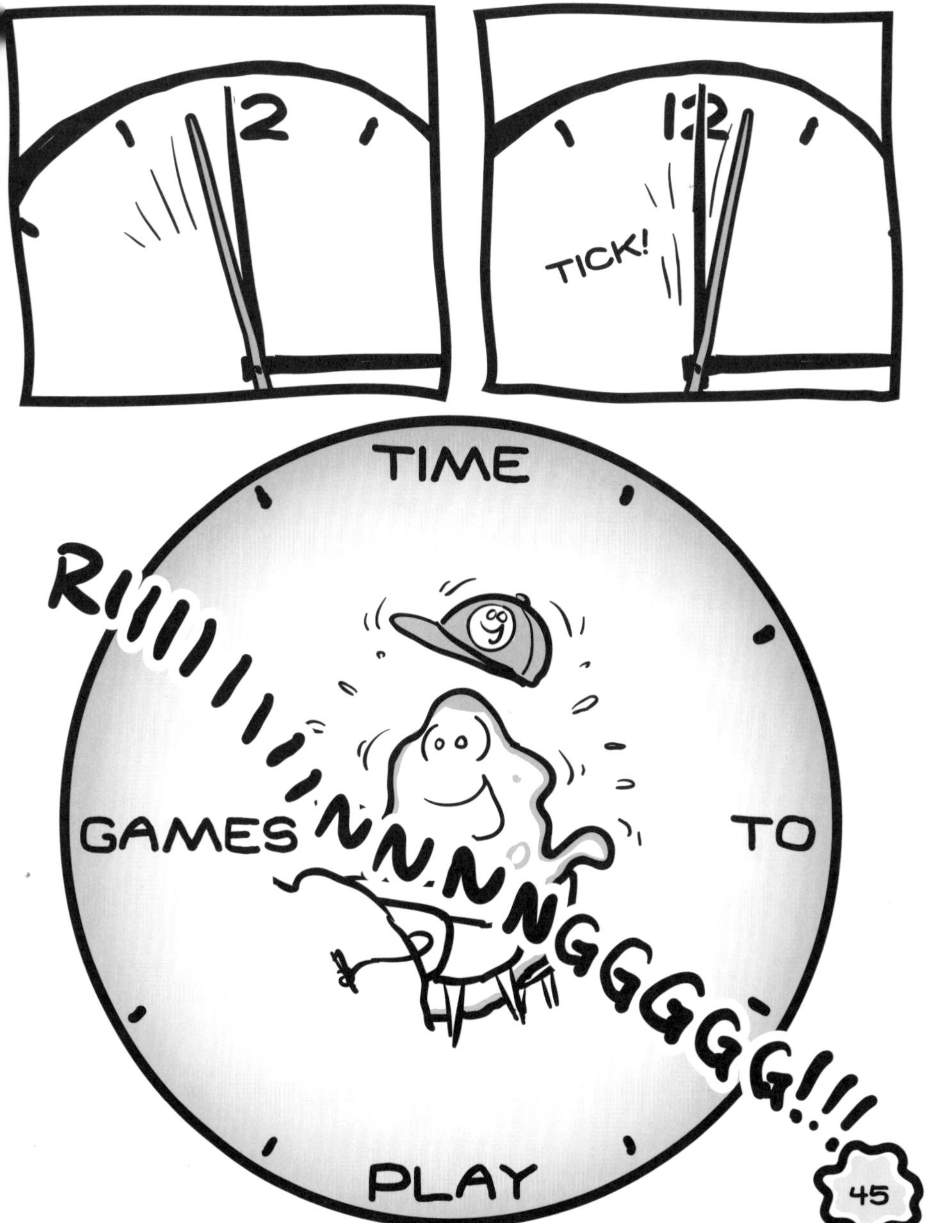
TICK!
TIME
GAMES
TO
PLAY
RIIIIIIIIINNNNNGGGGGG!!!

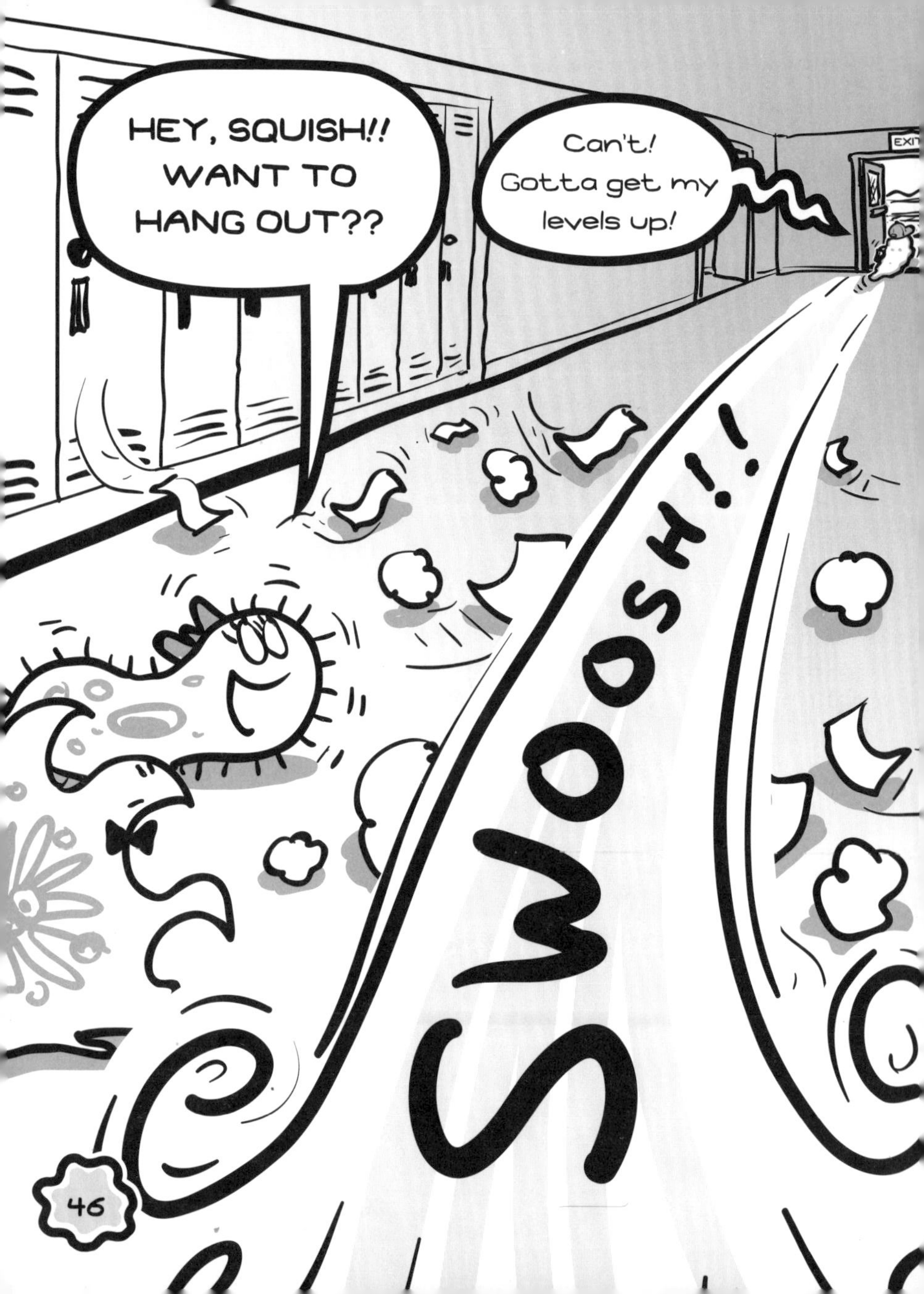
HEY, SQUISH!! WANT TO HANG OUT??
Can't! Gotta get my levels up!
EXIT
SWOOSH!!

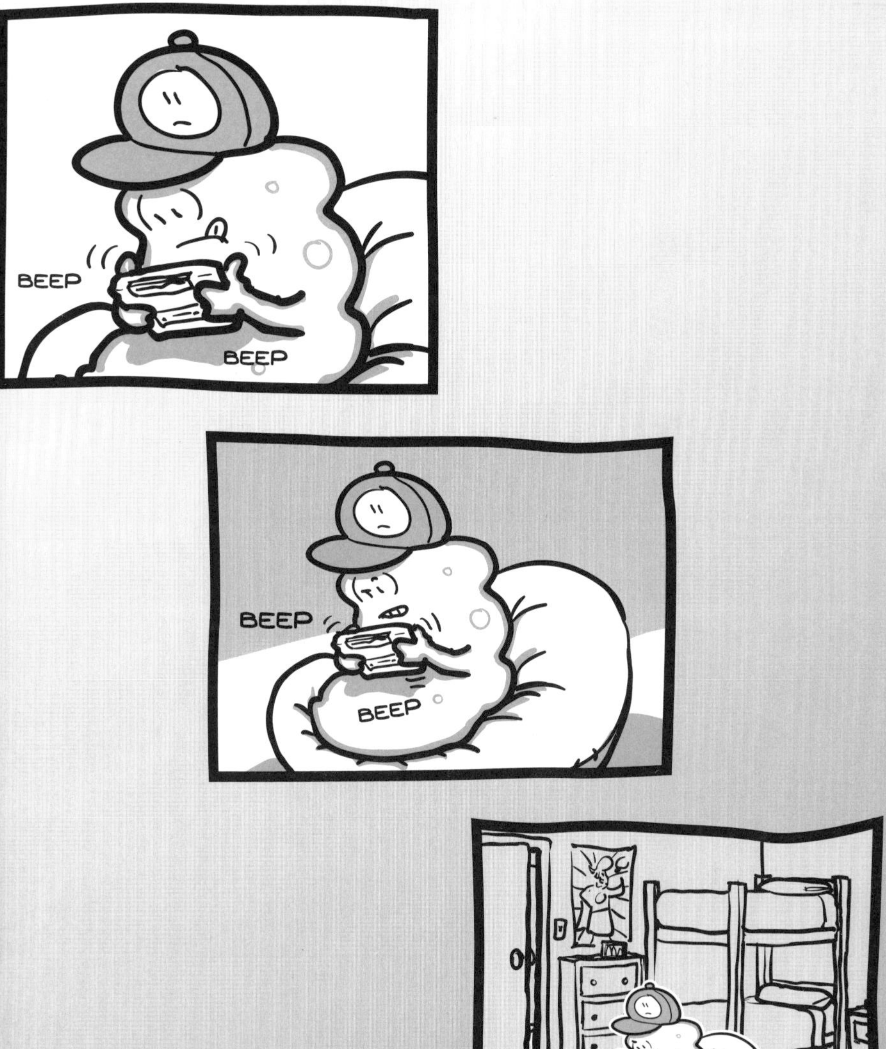
BEEP
BEEP
BEEP
BEEP
BEEP
BEEP

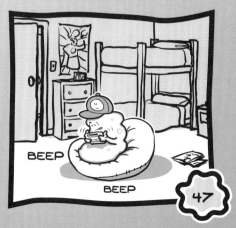

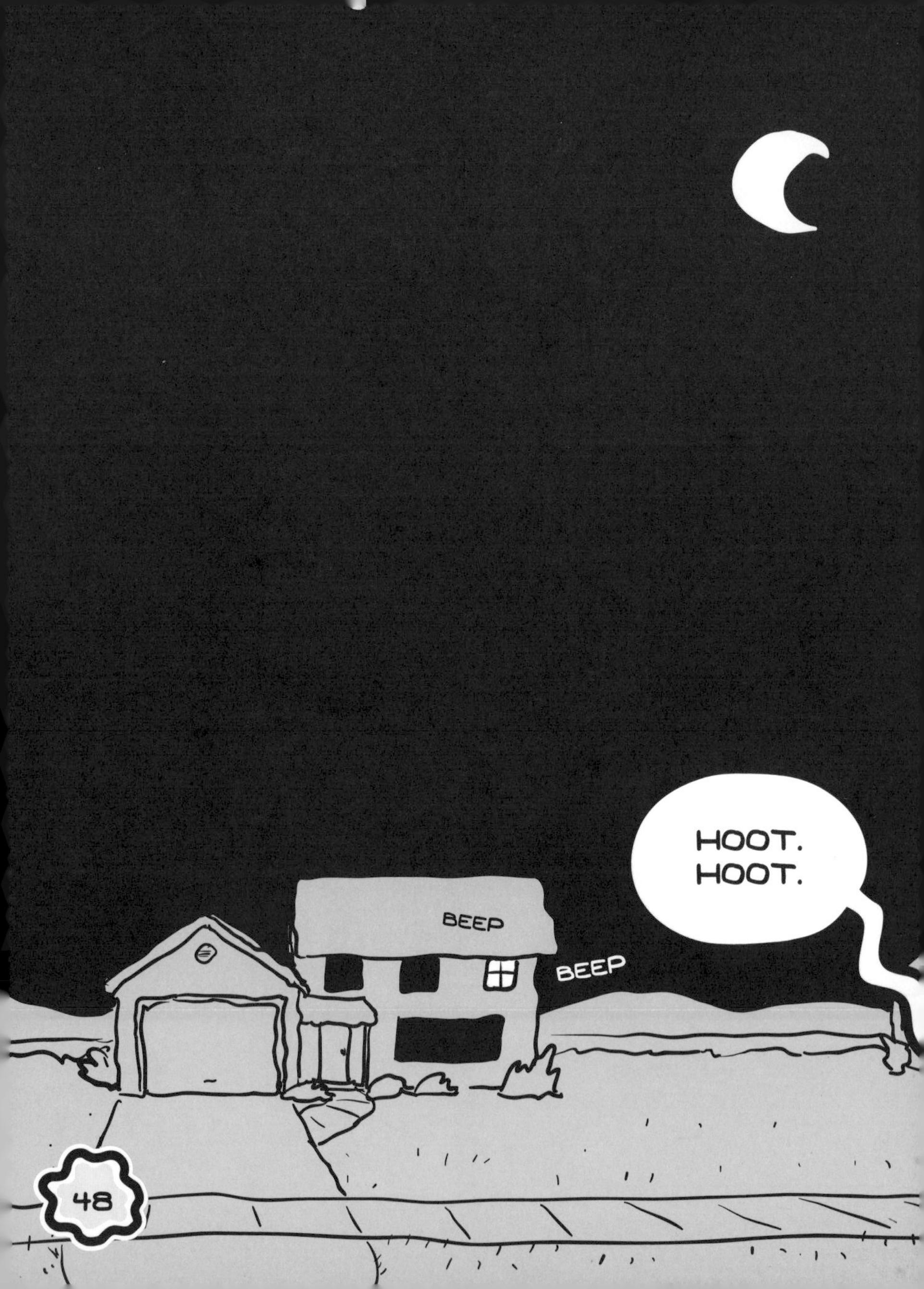
BEEP
BEEP
HOOT.
HOOT.

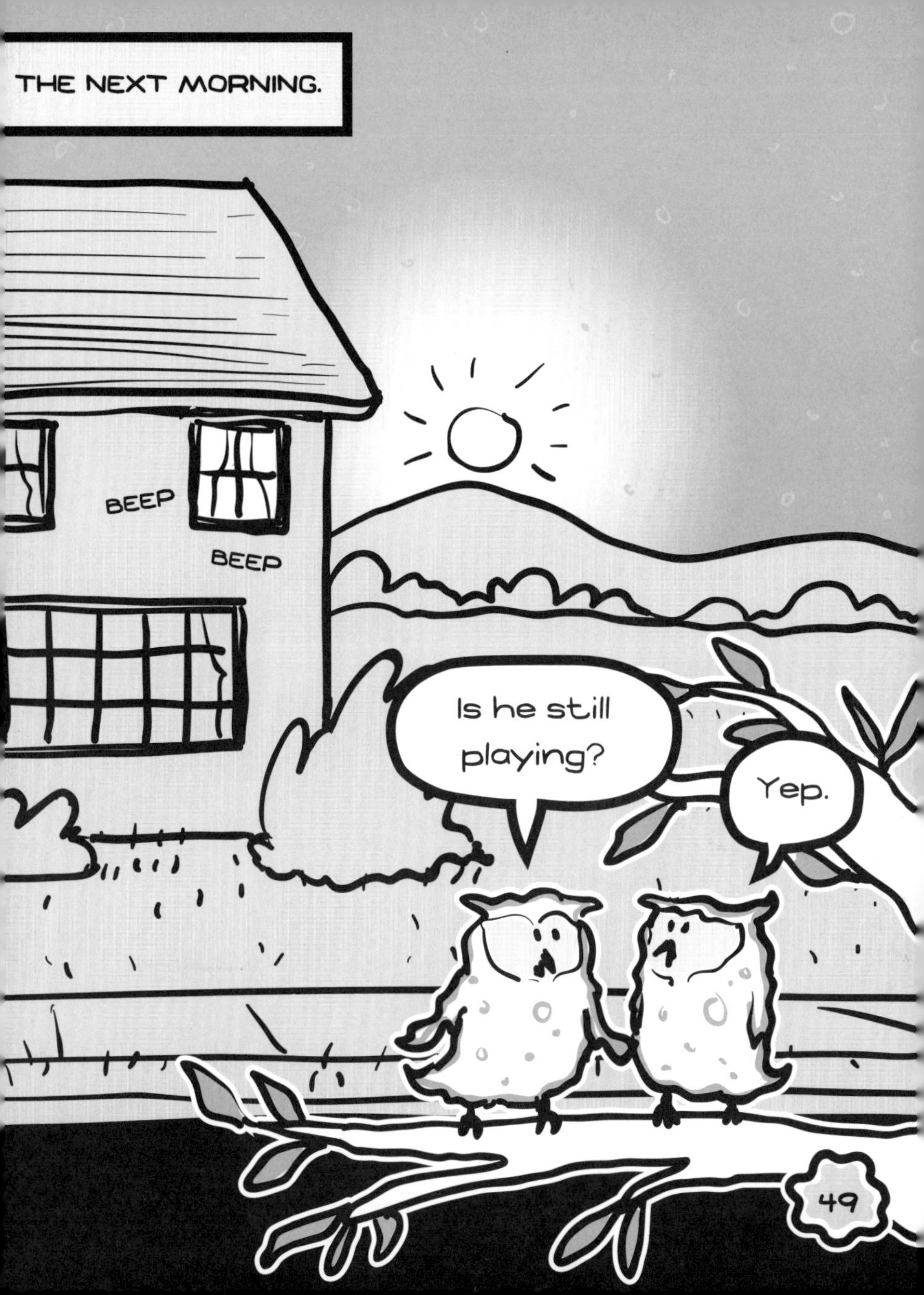
THE NEXT MORNING.
BEEP
BEEP
Is he still playing?
Yep.

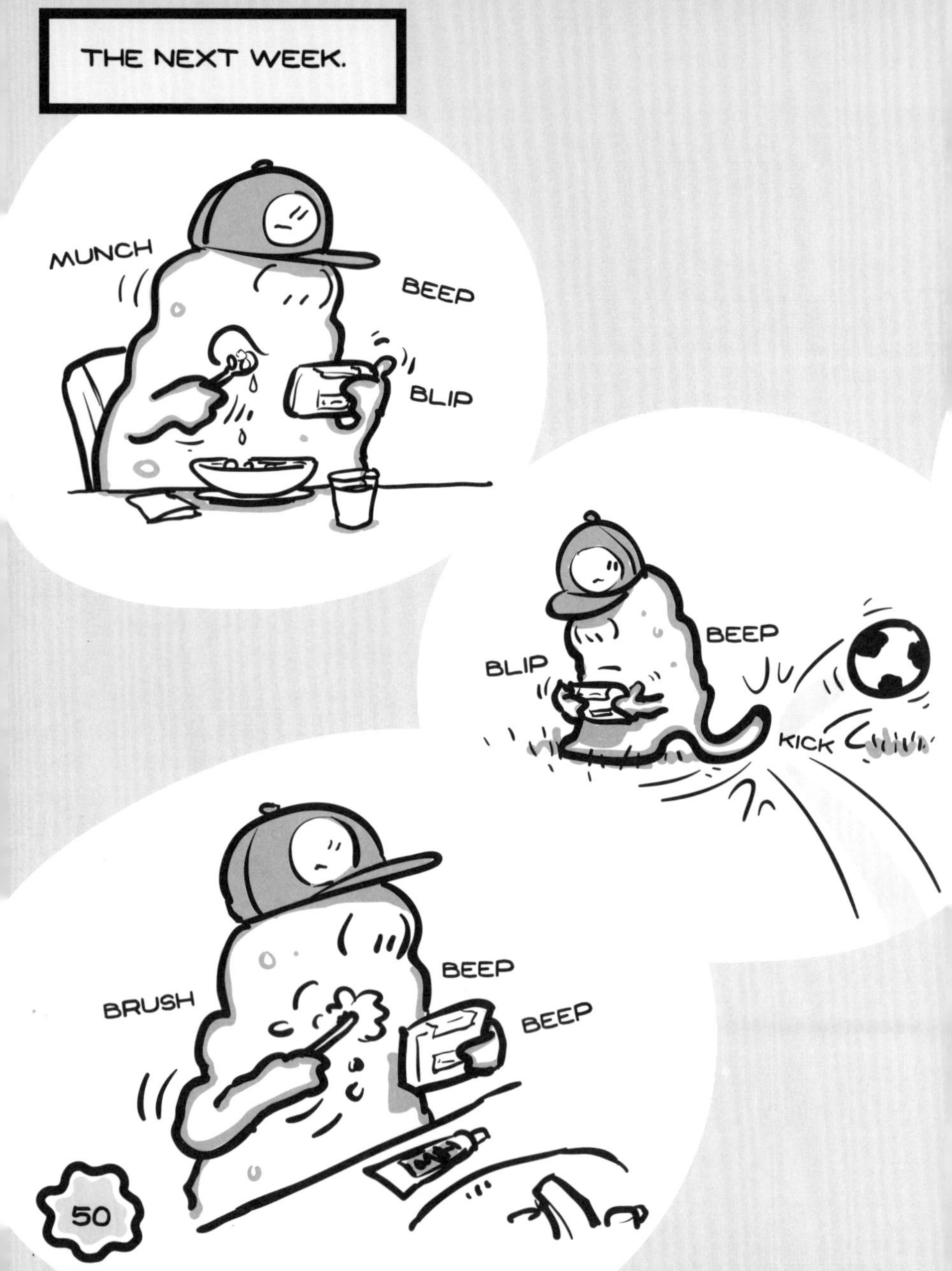
THE NEXT WEEK.
MUNCH
BEEP
BLIP
BEEP
BLIP
KICK
BRUSH
BEEP
BEEP

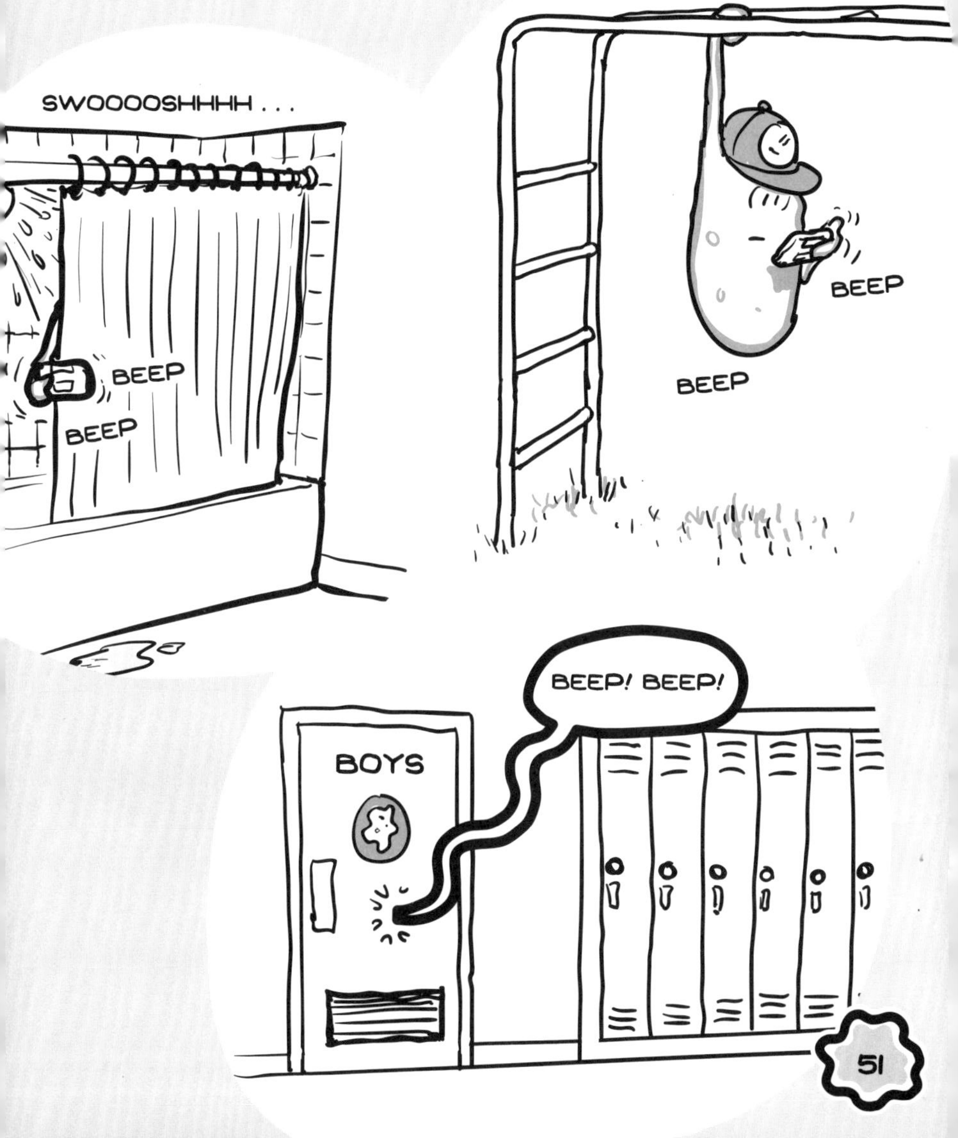
SWOOOOSHHHH . . .
BEEP
BEEP
BEEP
BEEP
BOYS
BEEP! BEEP!

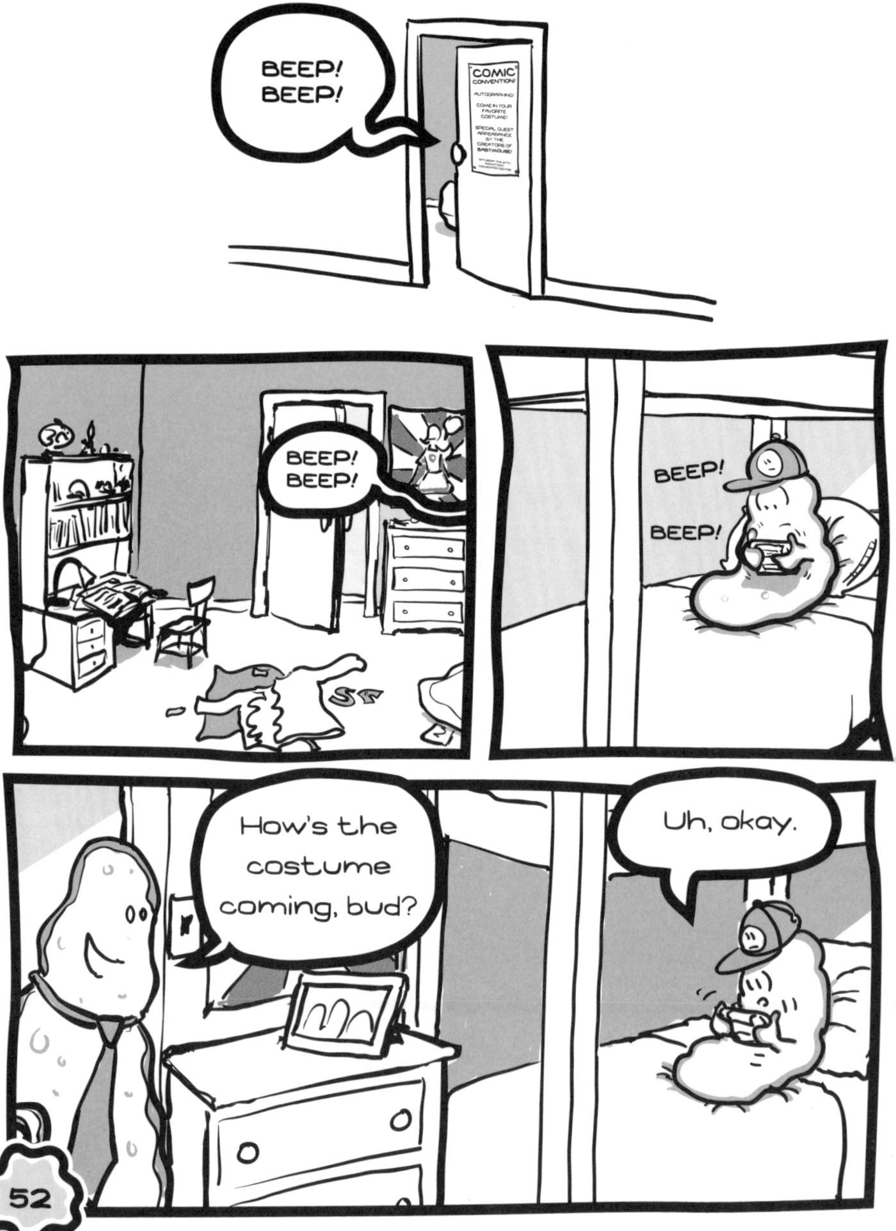
BEEP! BEEP!
COMIC CONVENTION!
AUTOGRAPHING!
COME IN YOUR FAVORITE COSTUME!
SPECIAL GUEST APPEARANCE BY THE CREATORS OF BABYMOUSE!
BEEP! BEEP!
BEEP!
BEEP!
How's the costume coming, bud?
Uh, okay.

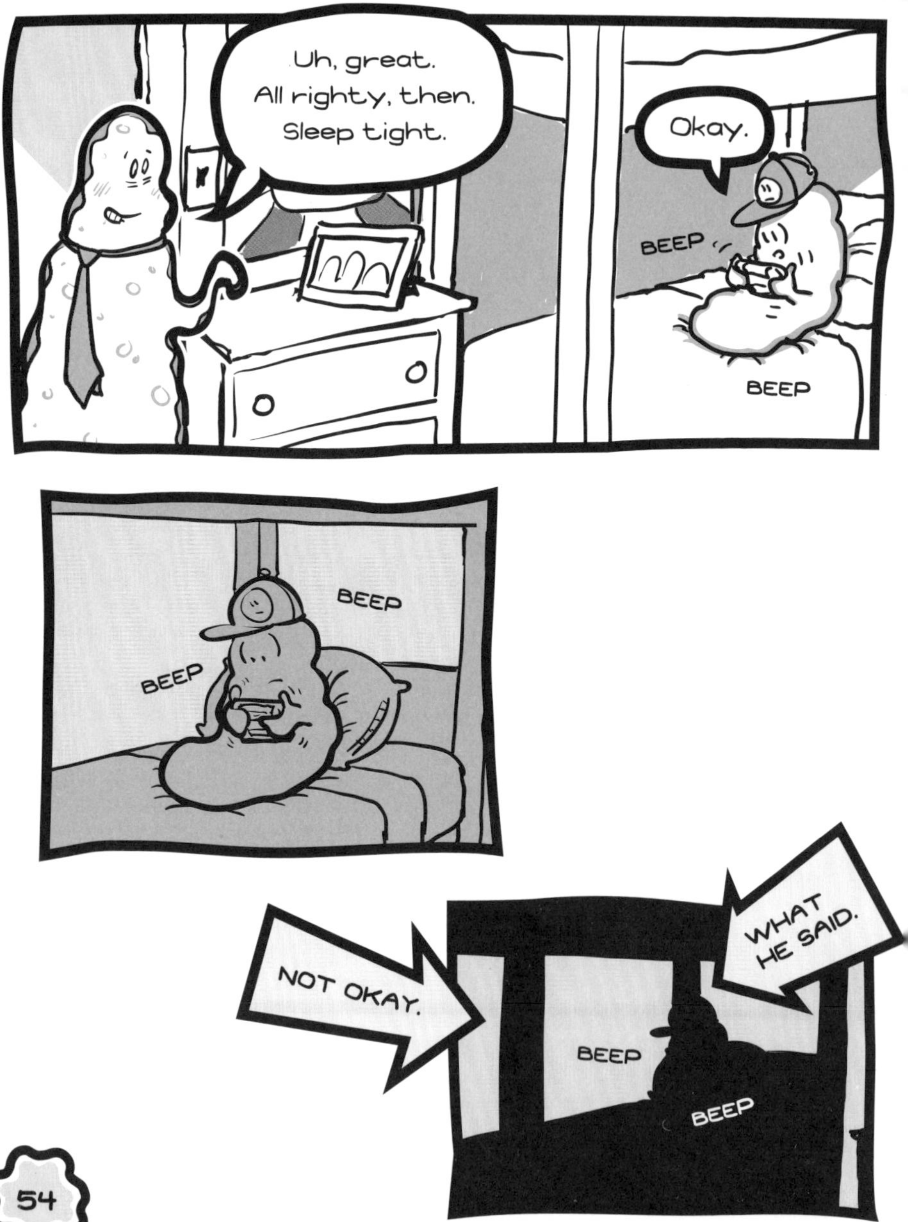
Uh, great.
All righty, then.
Sleep tight.
Okay.
BEEP
BEEP
BEEP
BEEP
NOT OKAY.
WHAT HE SAID.
BEEP
BEEP

EIGHTY-ONE HOURS OF GAME PLAY LATER.

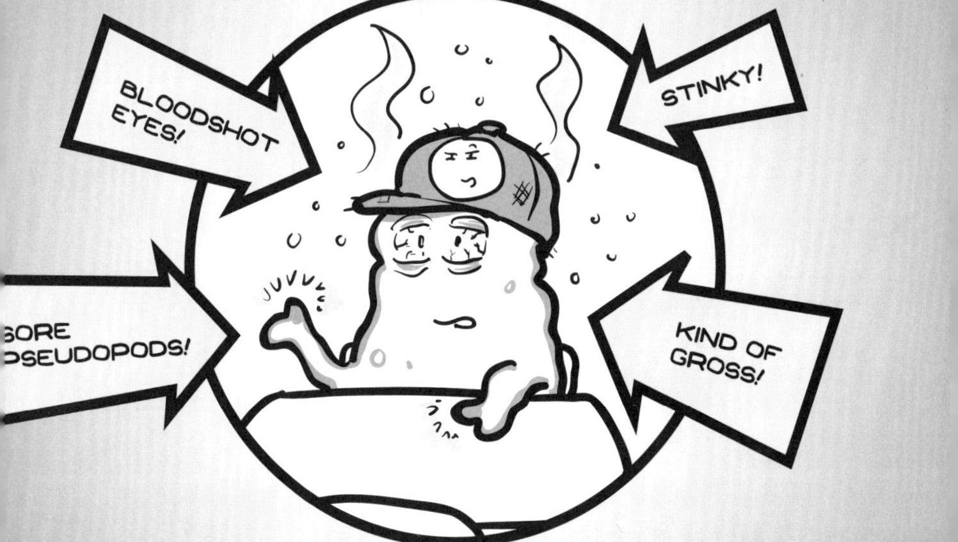
BLOODSHOT EYES!
STINKY!
SORE PSEUDOPODS!
KIND OF GROSS!

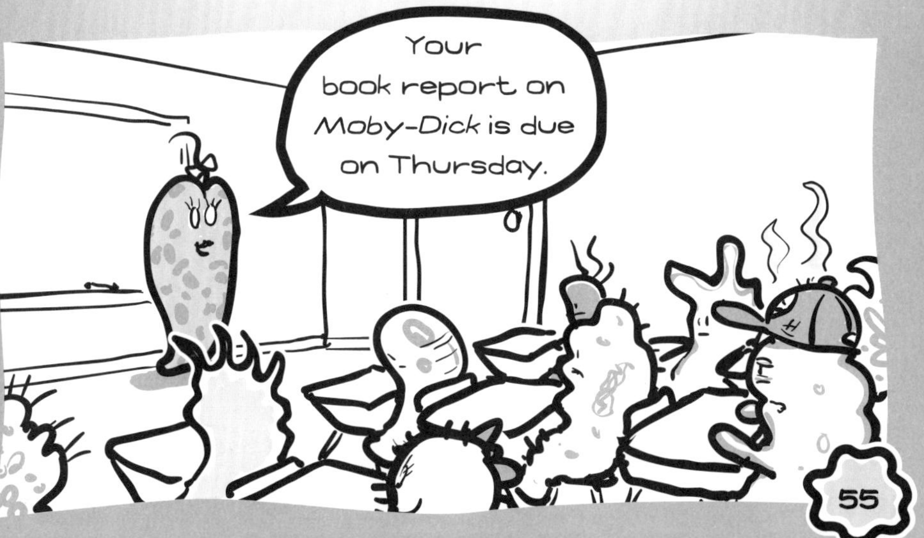
Your book report on *Moby-Dick* is due on Thursday.

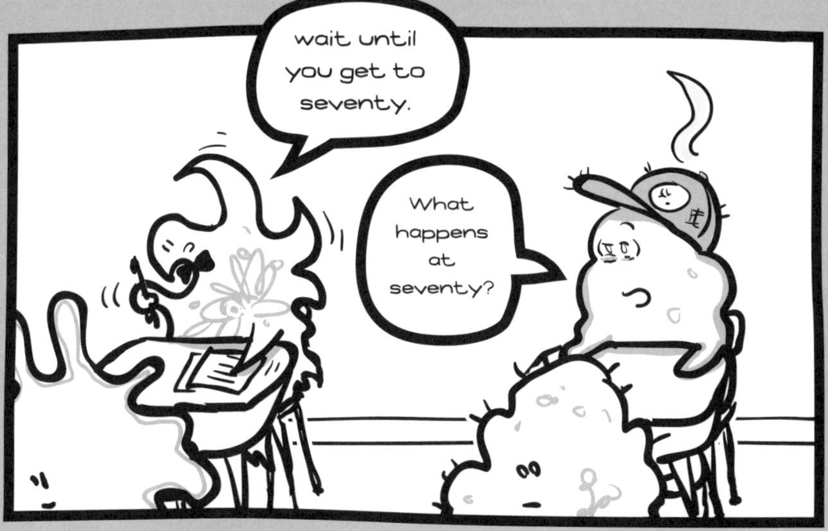
wait until you get to seventy.
What happens at seventy?
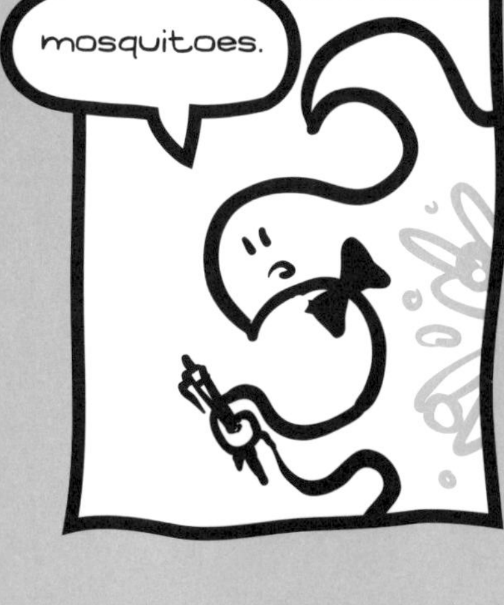
mosquitoes.
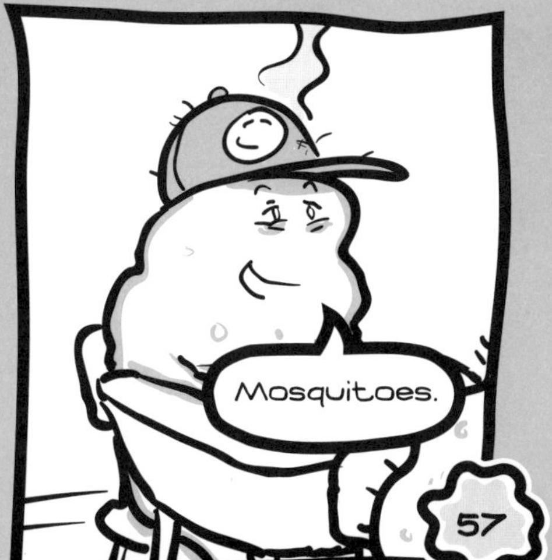
Mosquitoes.

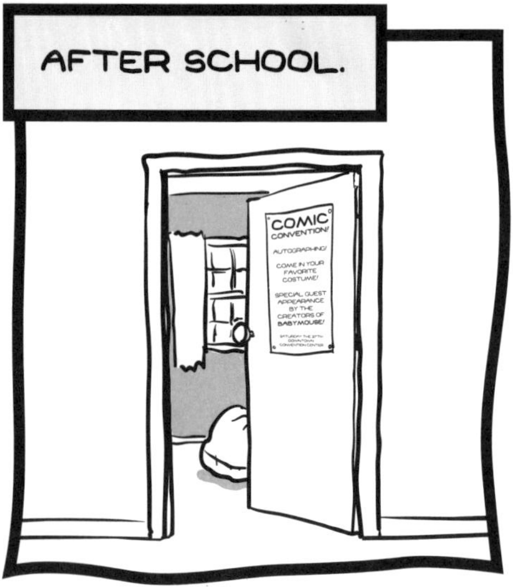
AFTER SCHOOL.
COMIC CONVENTION!
AUTOGRAPHING!
COME IN YOUR FAVORITE COSTUME!
SPECIAL GUEST APPEARANCE BY THE CREATORS OF BABYMOUSE!

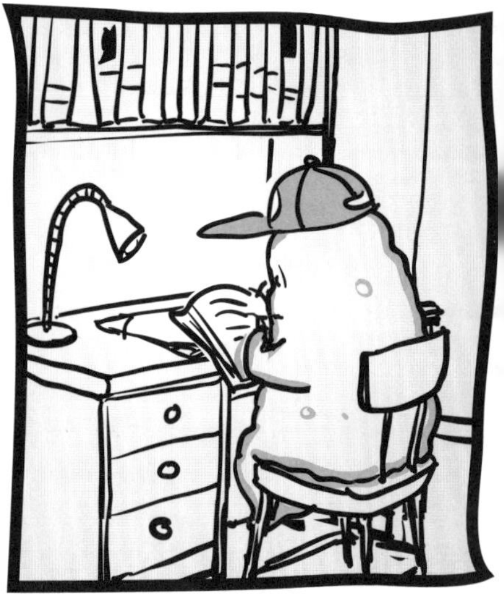

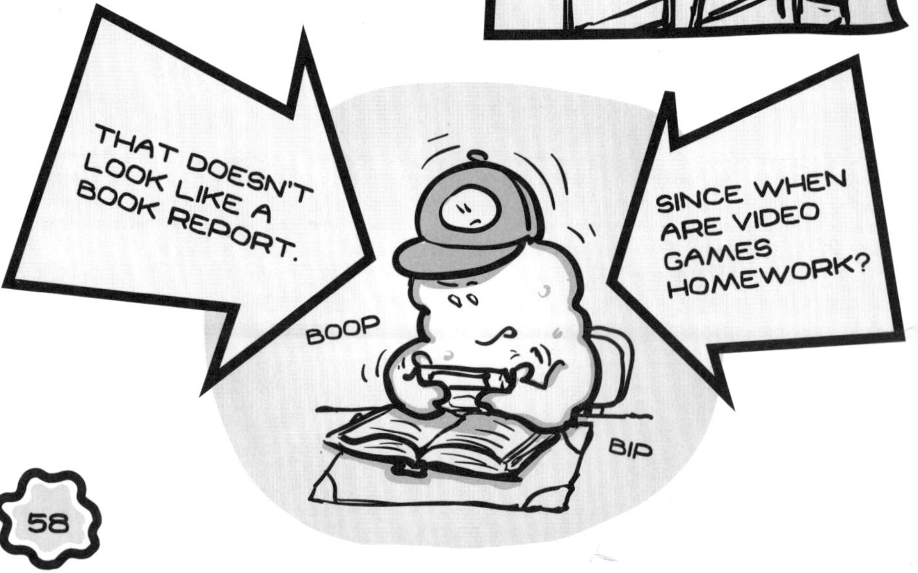
THAT DOESN'T LOOK LIKE A BOOK REPORT.
SINCE WHEN ARE VIDEO GAMES HOMEWORK?
BOOP
BIP

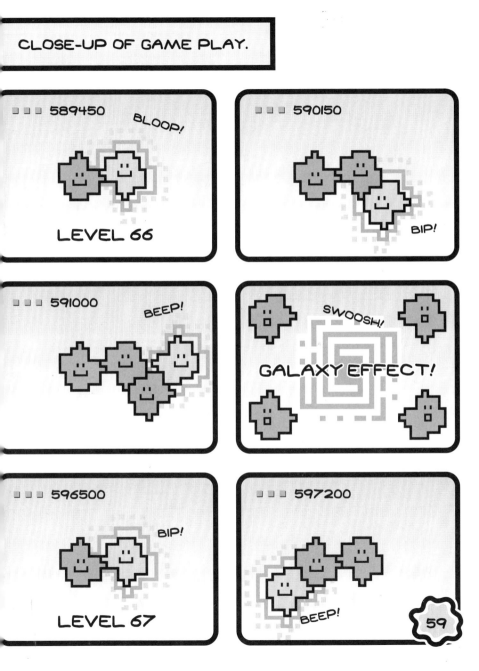

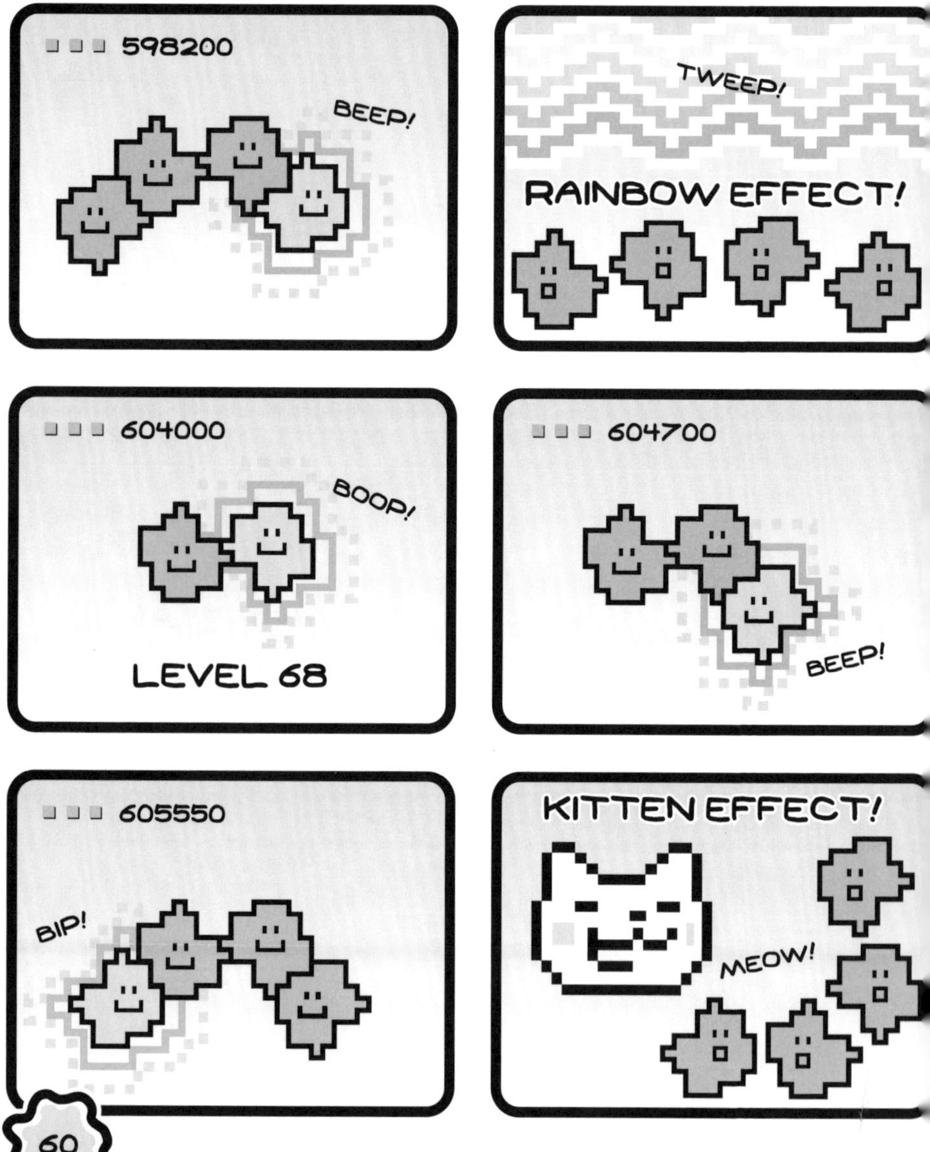
598200
BEEP!
TWEEP!
RAINBOW EFFECT!
604000
BOOP!
LEVEL 68
604700
BEEP!
605550
BIP!
KITTEN EFFECT!
MEOW!

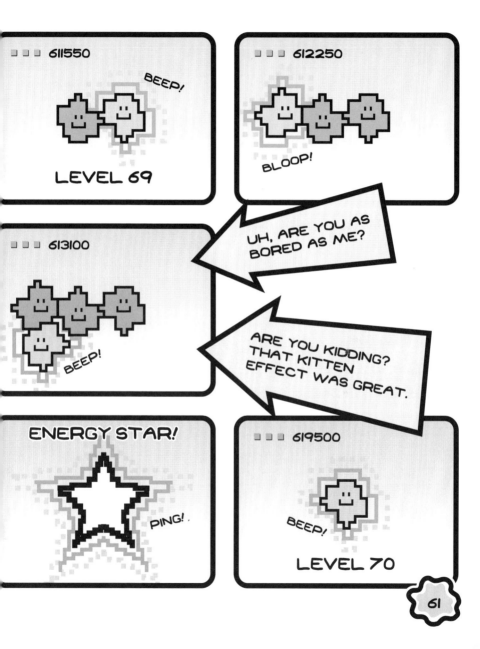

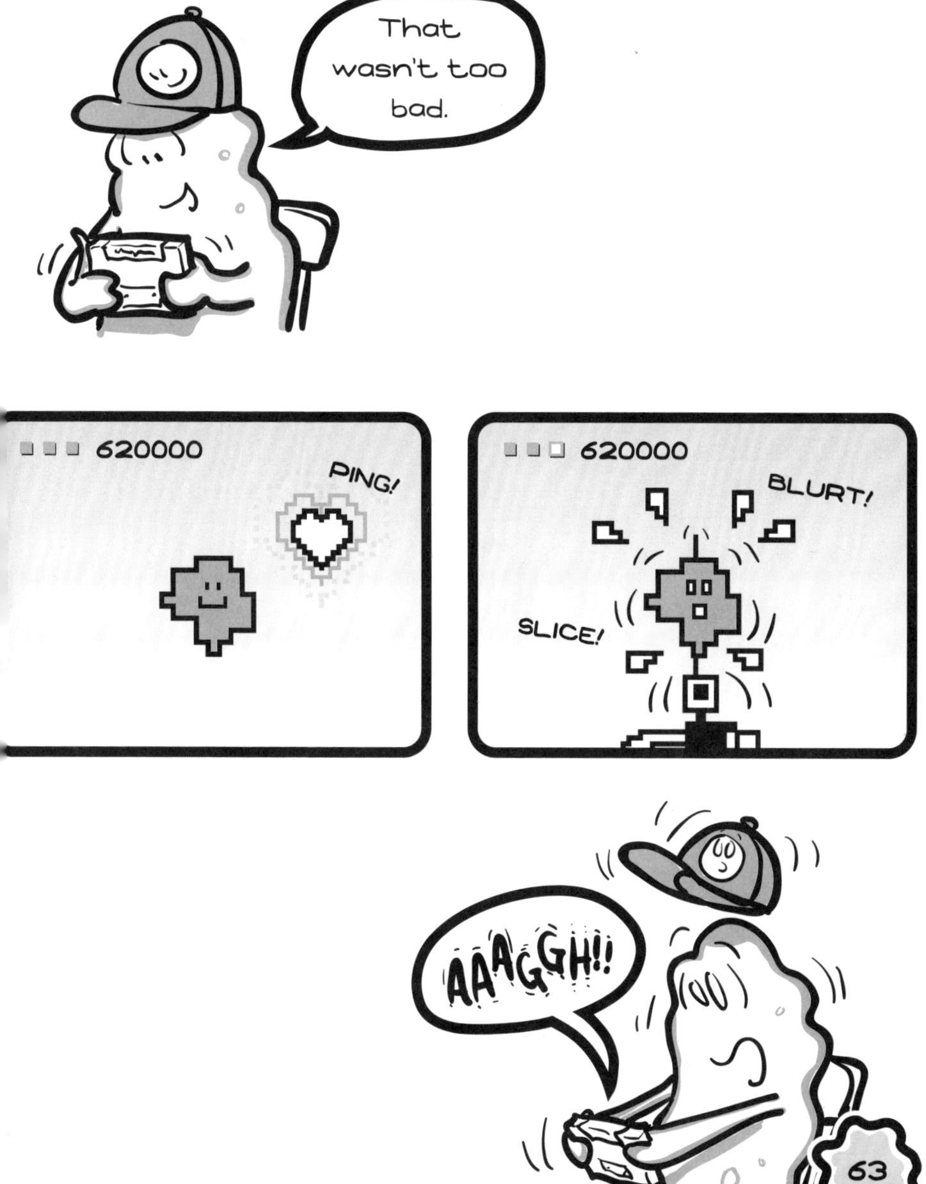
That wasn't too bad.
620000
PING!
620000
BLURT!
SLICE!
AAAGGH!!

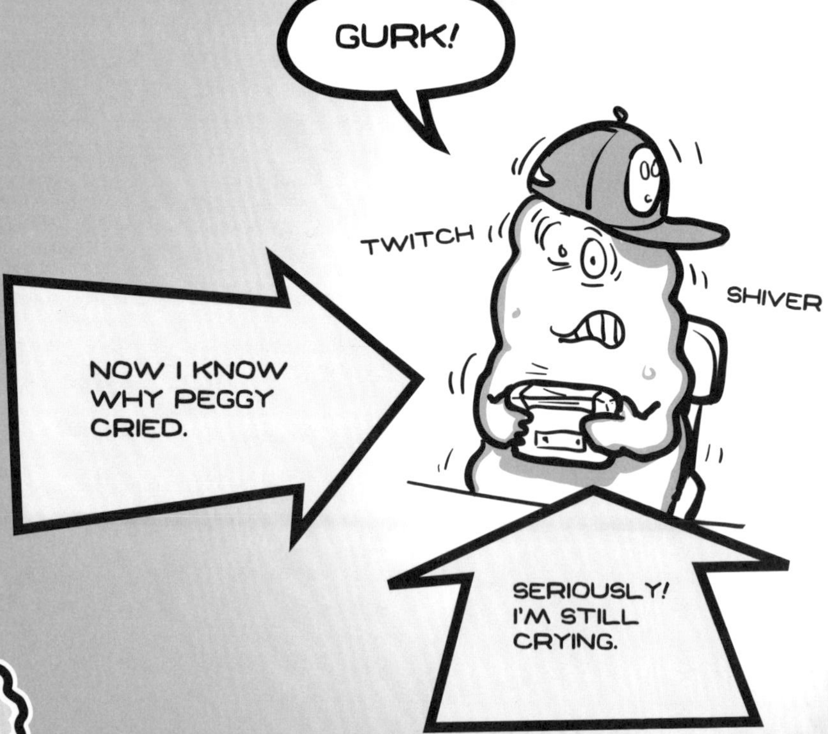
GURK!
TWITCH
SHIVER
NOW I KNOW WHY PEGGY CRIED.
SERIOUSLY! I'M STILL CRYING.

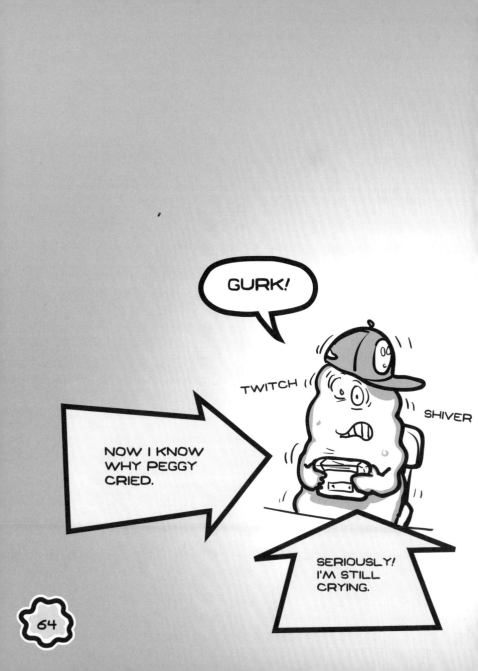

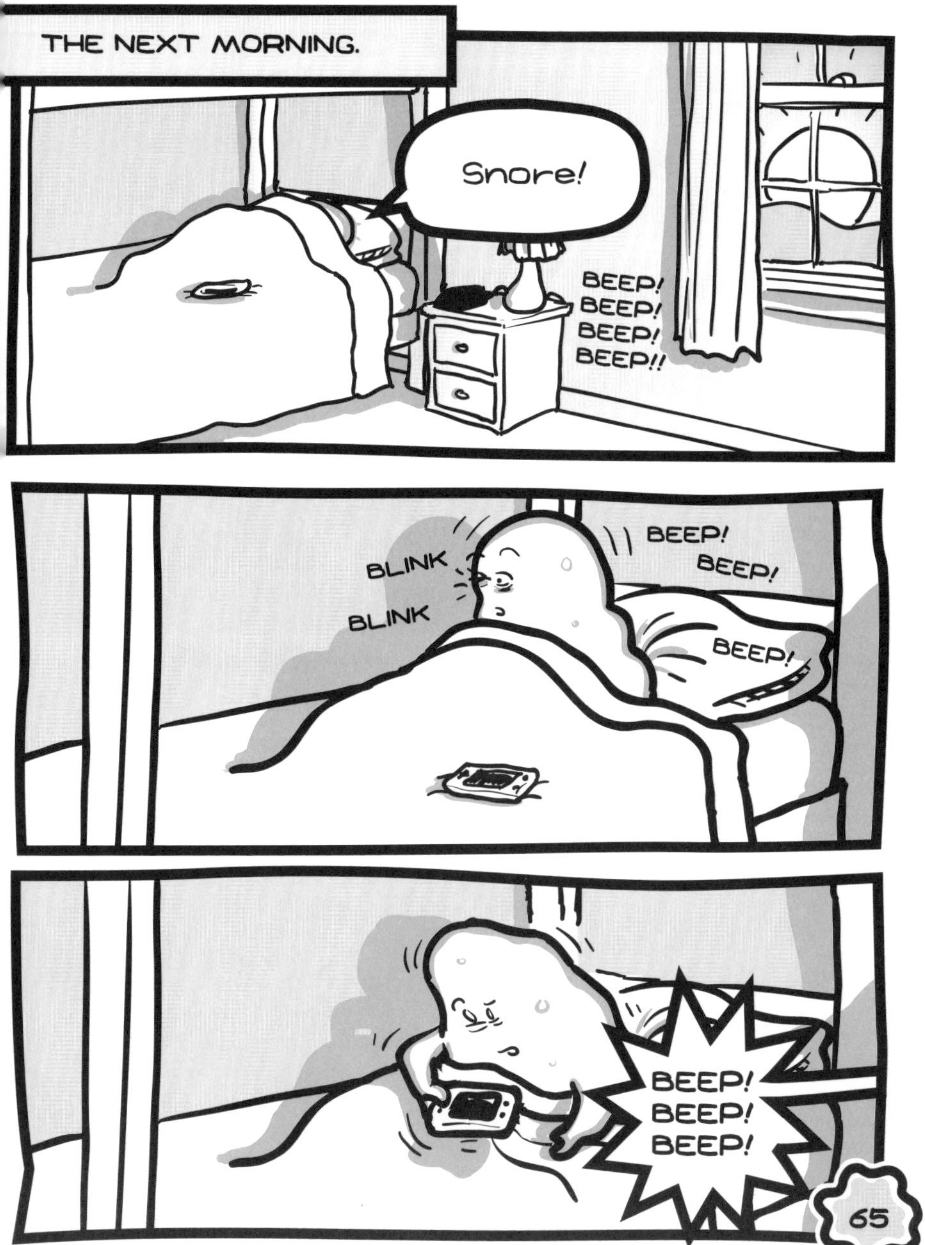
THE NEXT MORNING.
Snore!
BEEP! BEEP! BEEP! BEEP!!
BLINK
BLINK
BEEP!
BEEP!
BEEP!
BEEP! BEEP! BEEP!

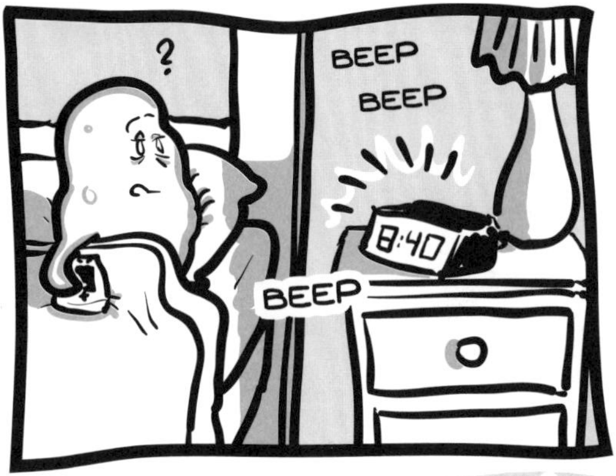
?
BEEP
BEEP
8:40
BEEP

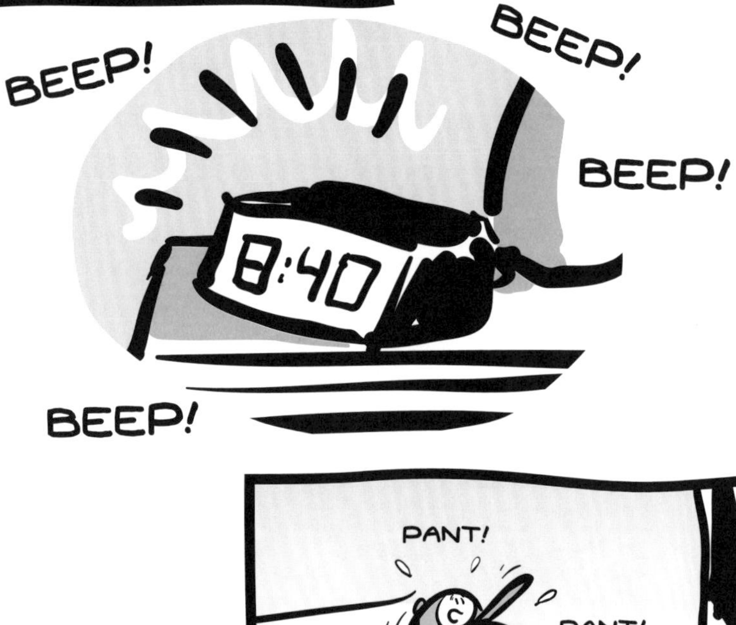
BEEP!
BEEP!
BEEP!
8:40
BEEP!

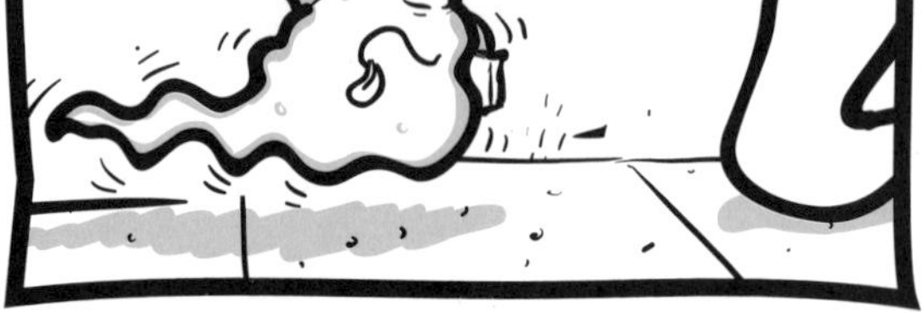
PANT!
PANT!

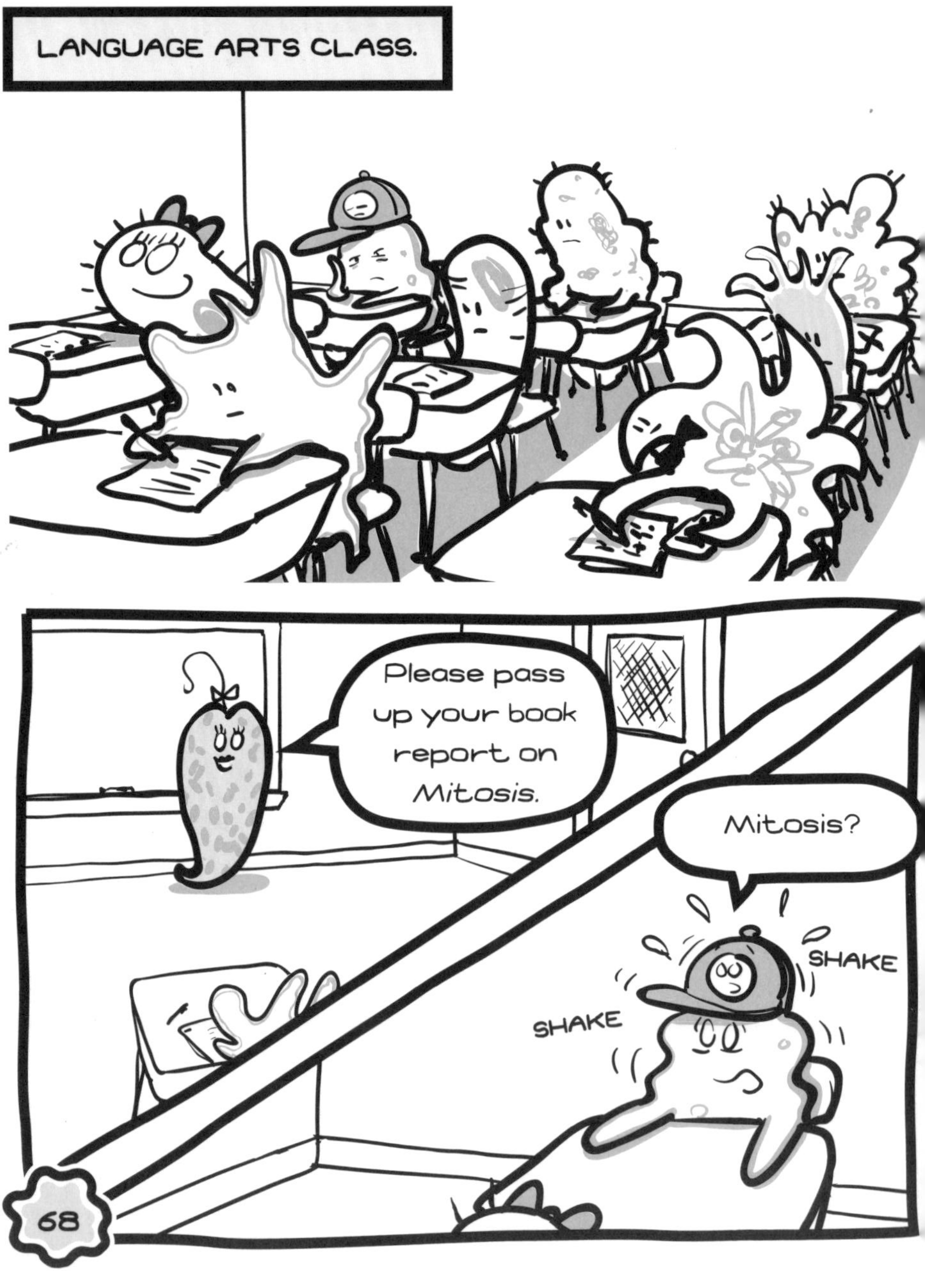
LANGUAGE ARTS CLASS.
Please pass up your book report on *Mitosis*.
Mitosis?
SHAKE
SHAKE

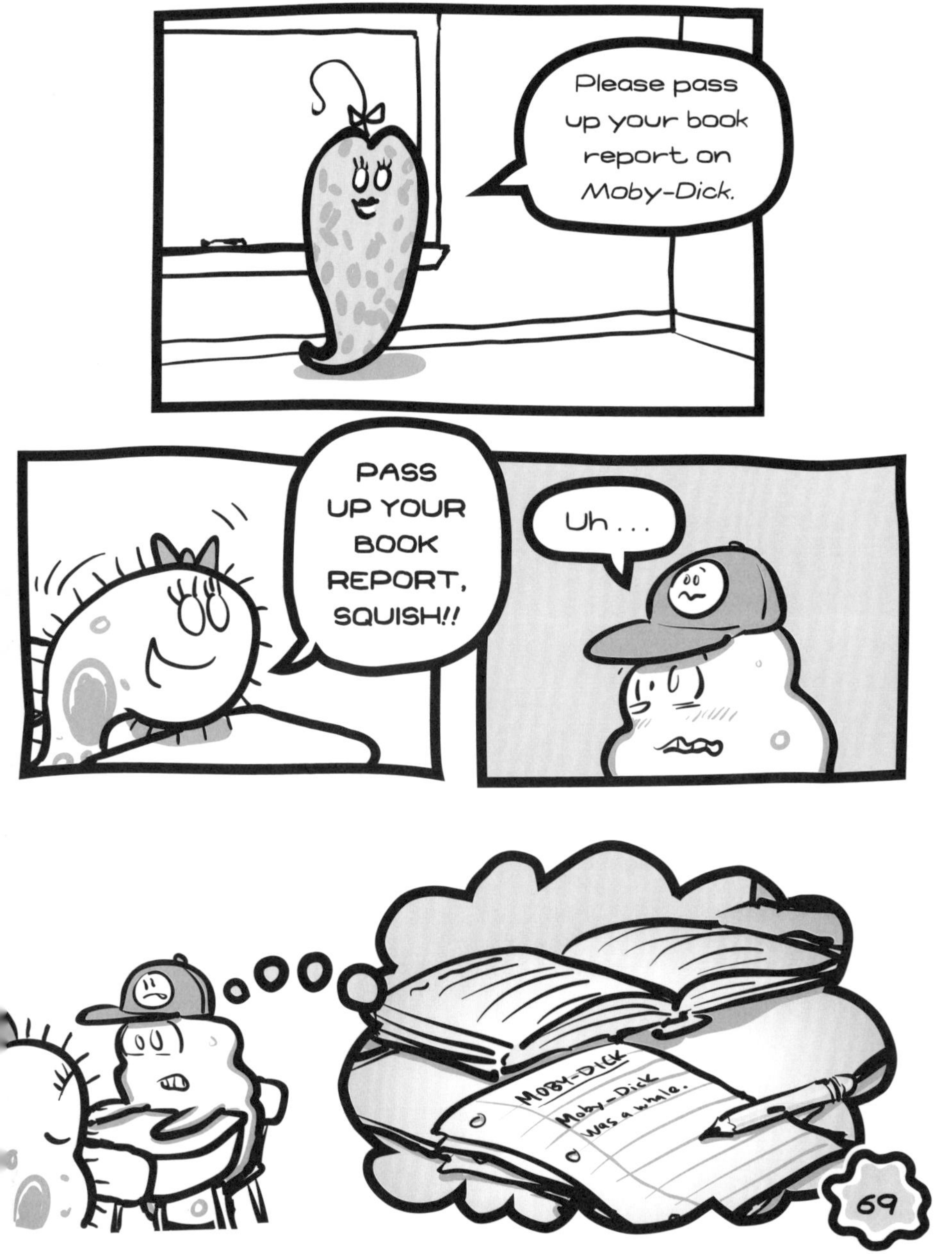
Please pass up your book report on Moby-Dick.
PASS UP YOUR BOOK REPORT, SQUISH!!
Uh . . .
MOBY-DICK
Moby-Dick was a whale.

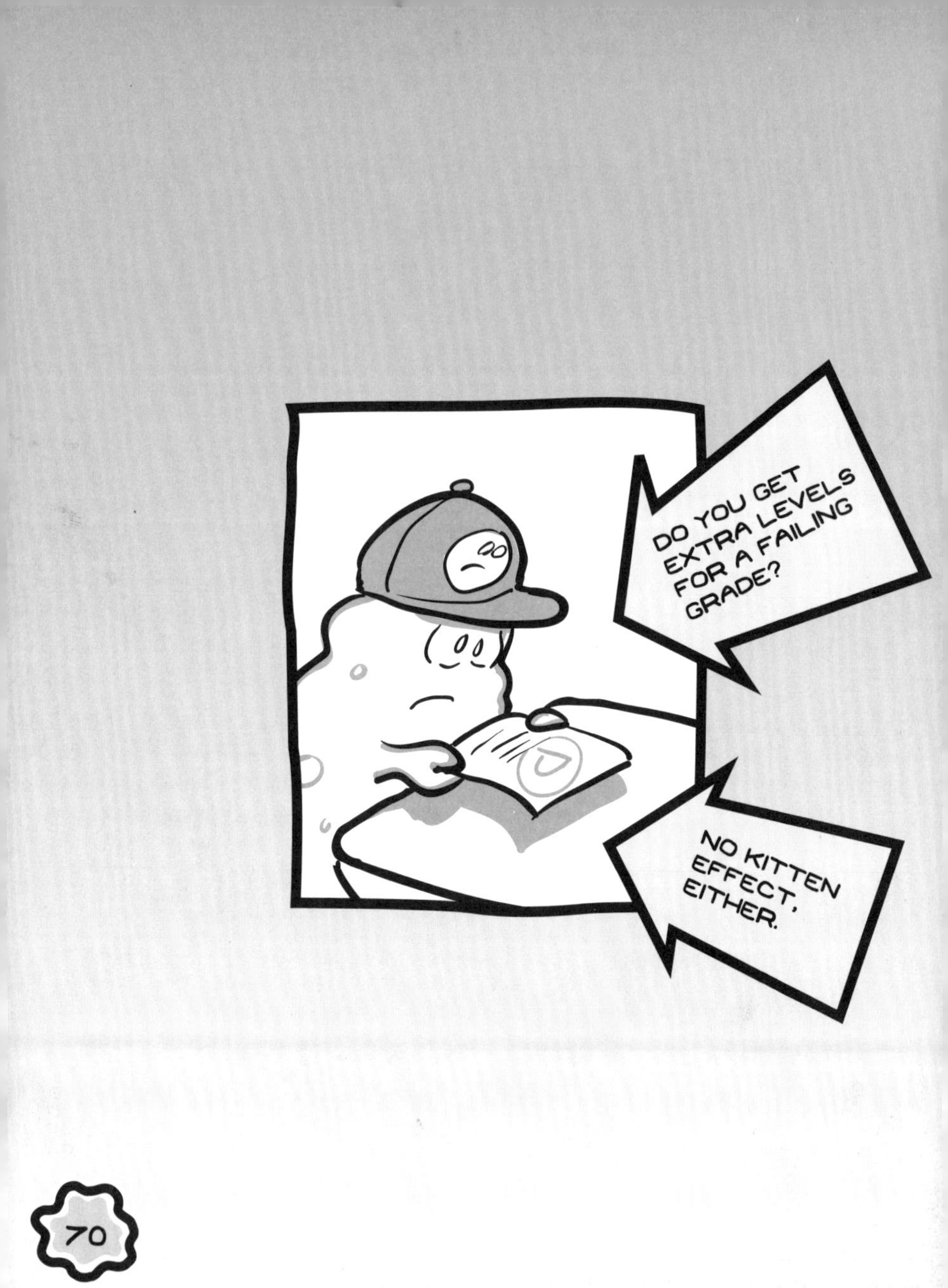
DO YOU GET EXTRA LEVELS FOR A FAILING GRADE?
NO KITTEN EFFECT, EITHER.

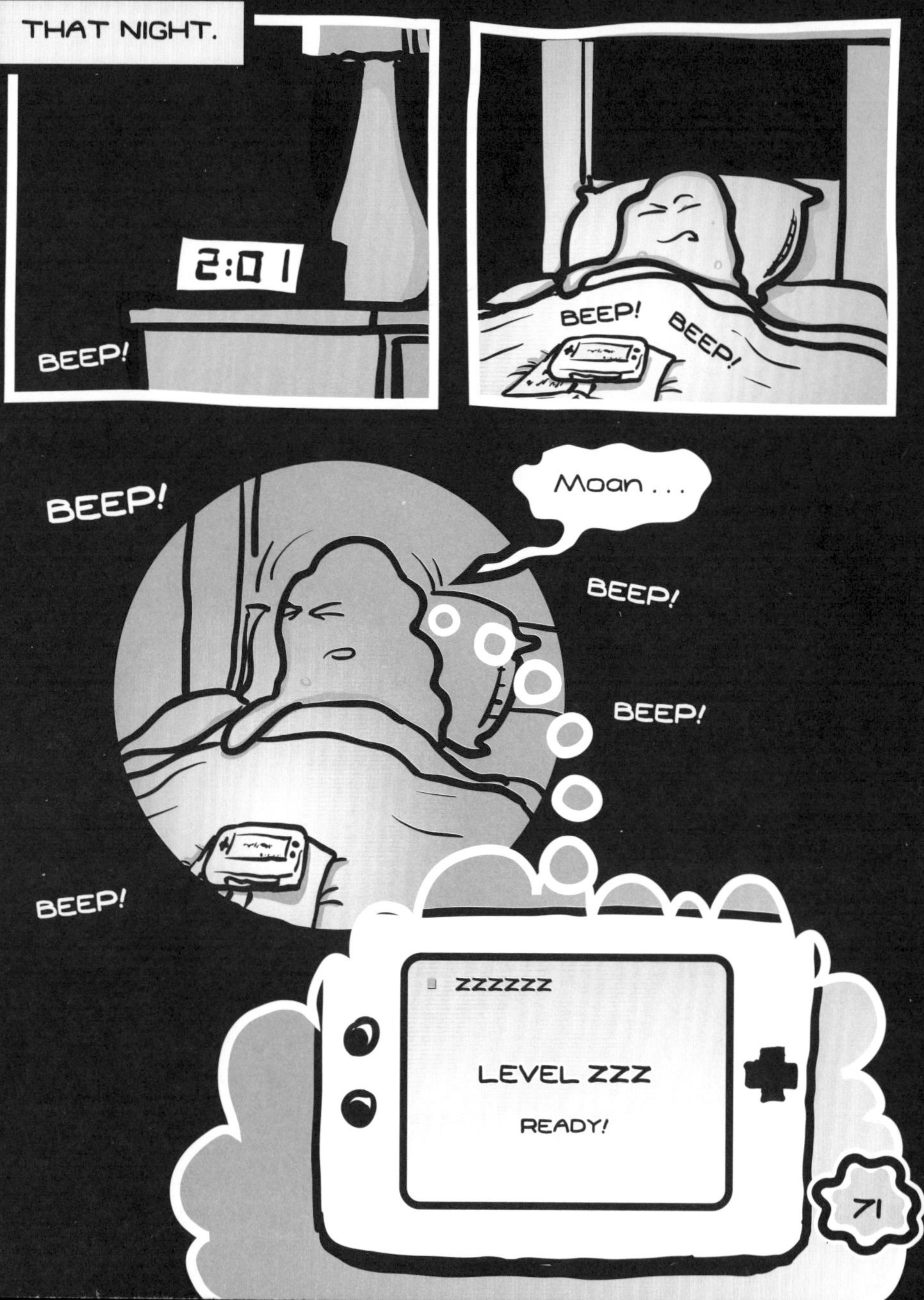

THAT NIGHT.
2:01
BEEP!
BEEP!
BEEP!
BEEP!
Moan . . .
BEEP!
BEEP!
BEEP!
ZZZZZZ
LEVEL ZZZ
READY!

ZZZZZZ

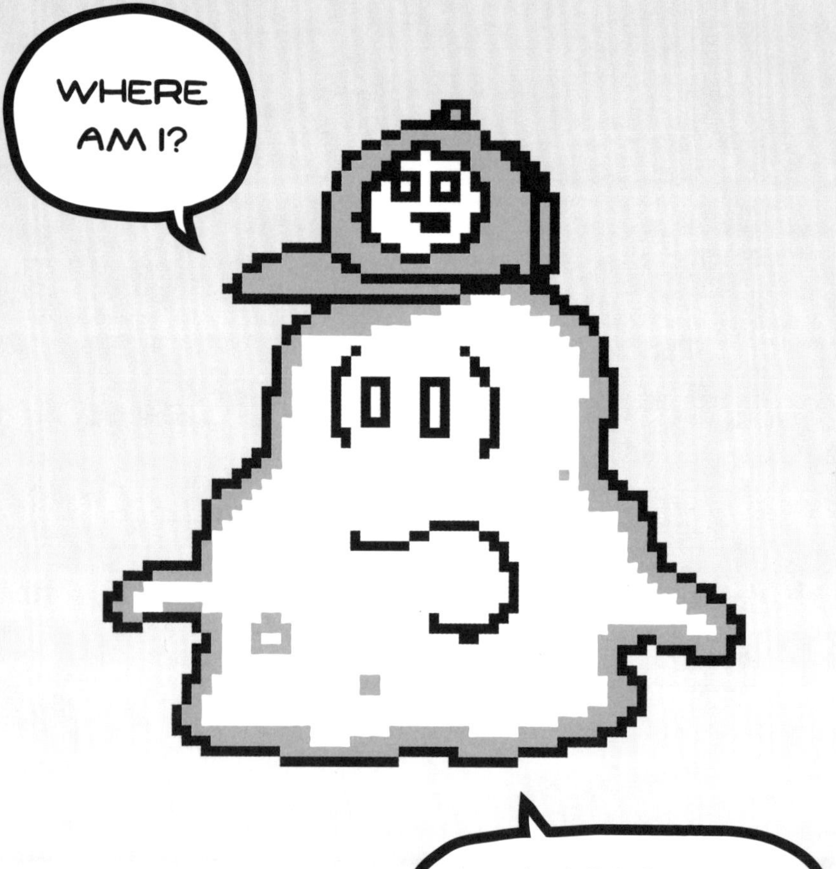
WHERE AM I?
WHY AM I PIXELATED?

LEVEL UP!

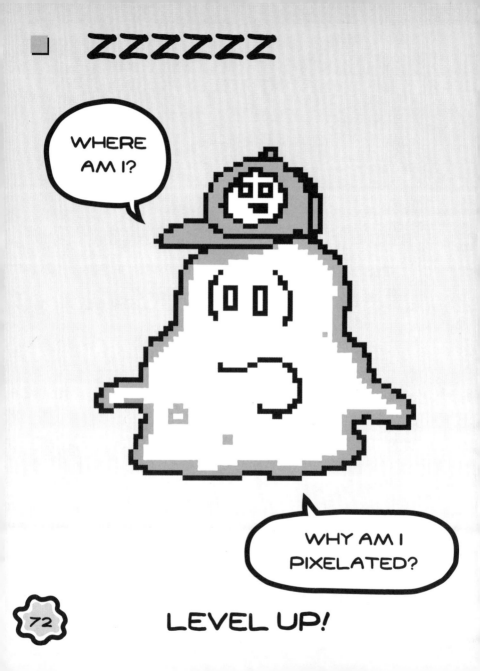

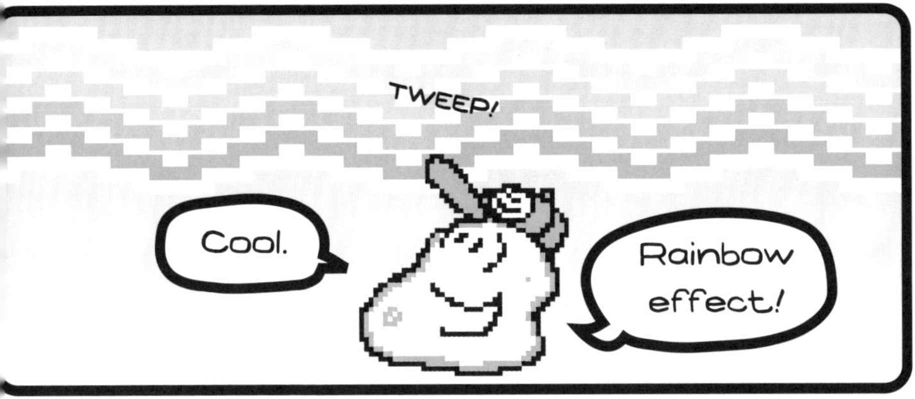
TWEEP!
Cool.
Rainbow effect!

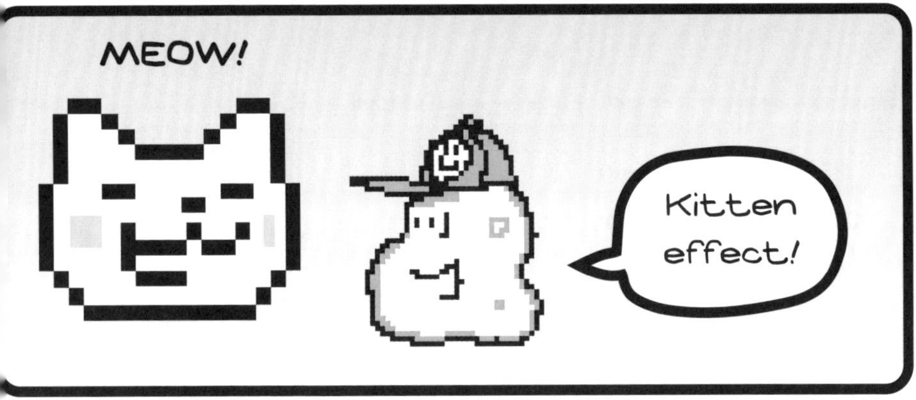
MEOW!
Kitten effect!

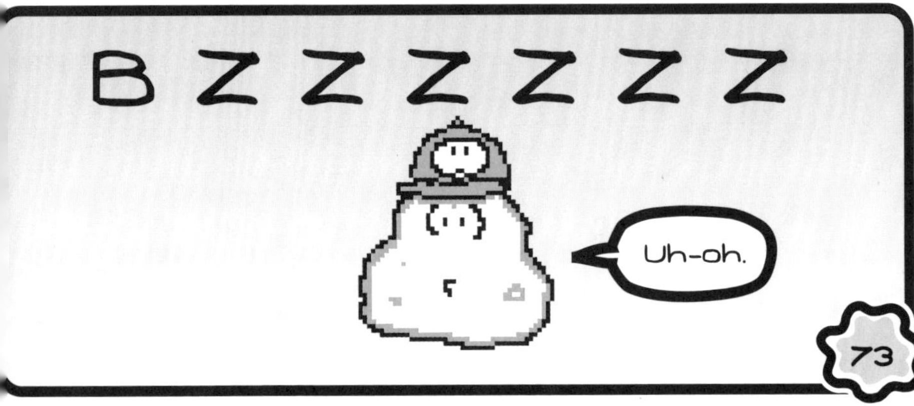
B Z Z Z Z Z Z
Uh-oh.

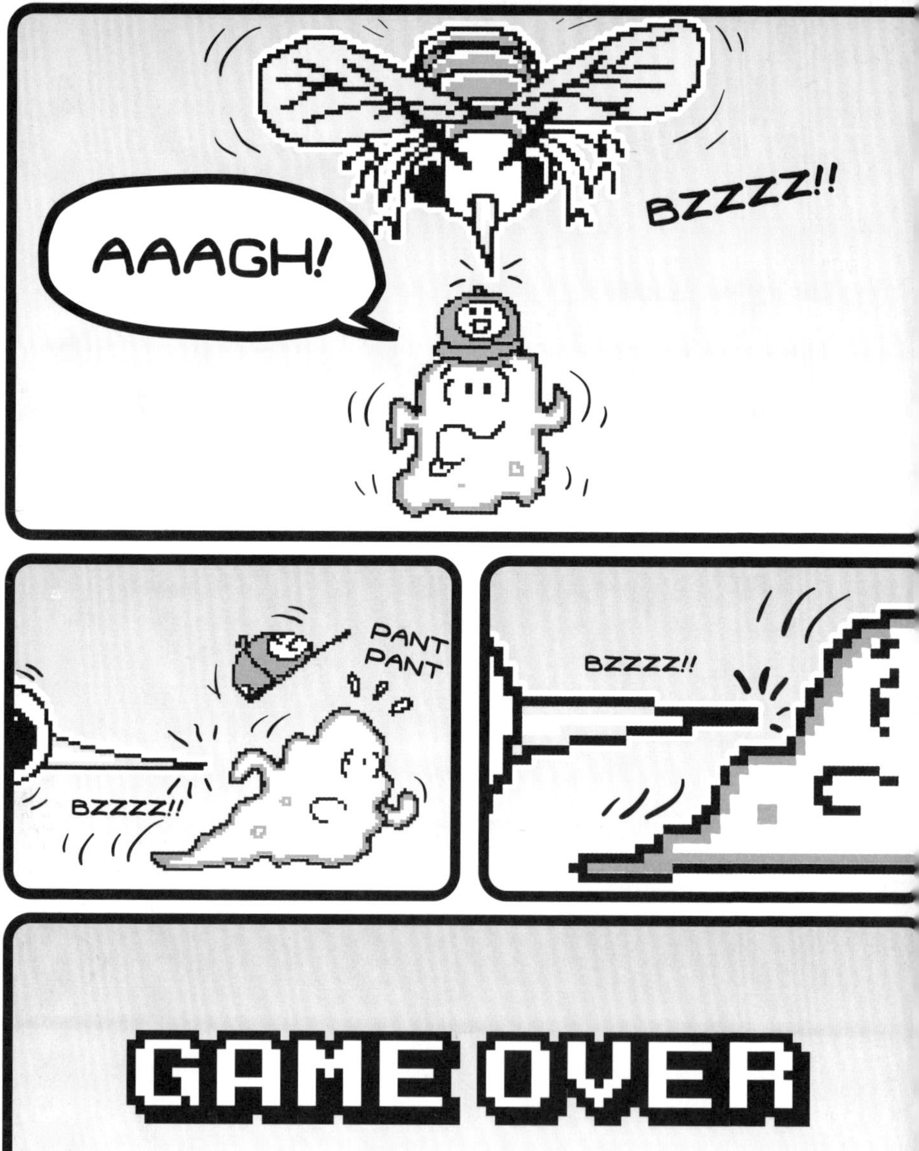
AAAGH!
BZZZZ!!
PANT
PANT
BZZZZ!!
BZZZZ!!
GAME OVER

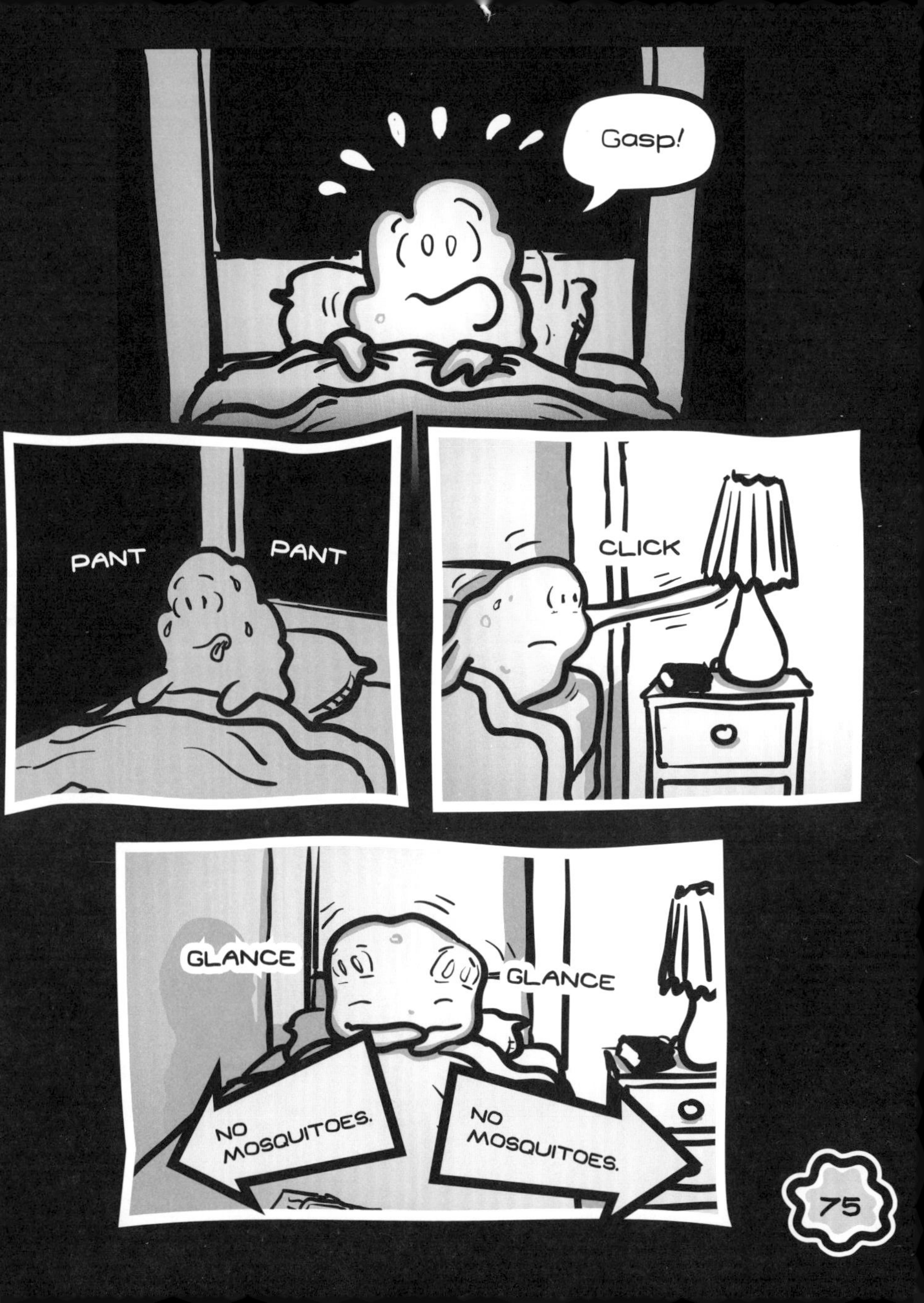

Gasp!
PANT
PANT
CLICK
GLANCE
GLANCE
NO MOSQUITOES.
NO MOSQUITOES.

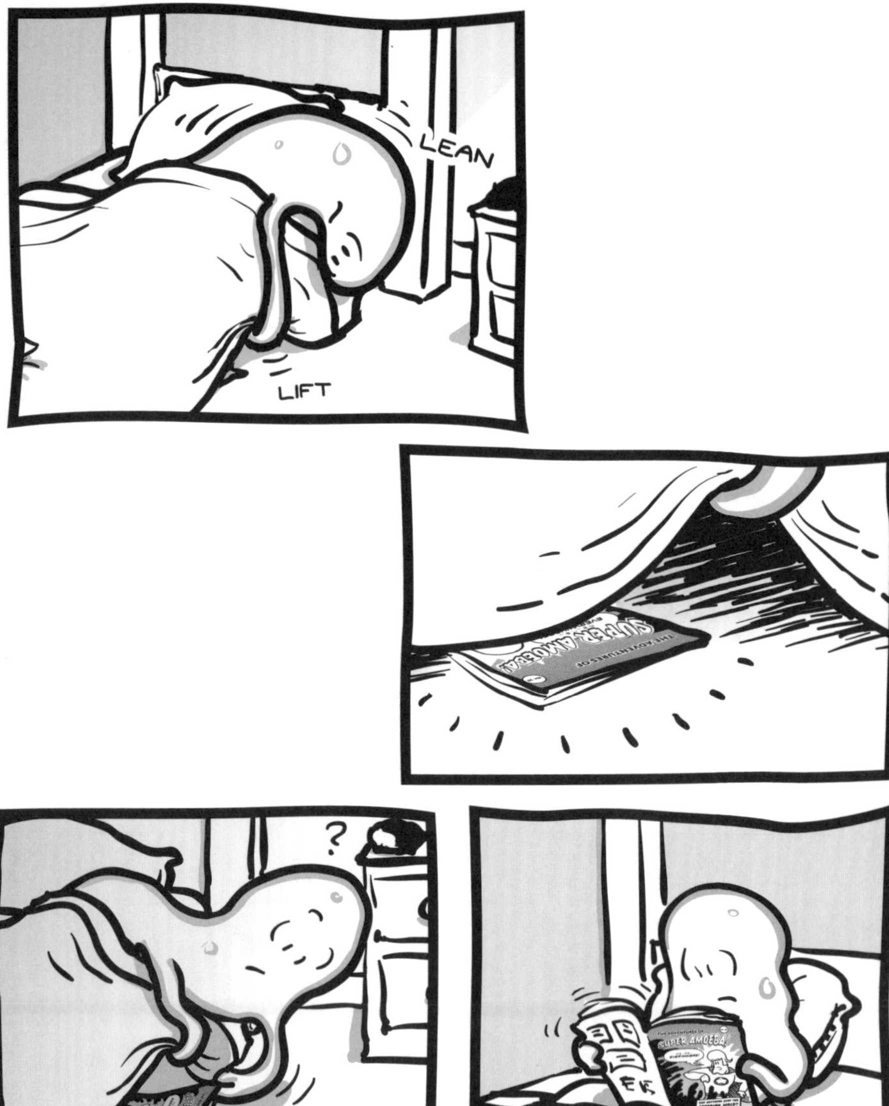
LEAN
LIFT
THE ADVENTURES OF
SUPER AMOEBA!
?
THE ADVENTURES OF
SUPER AMOEBA!

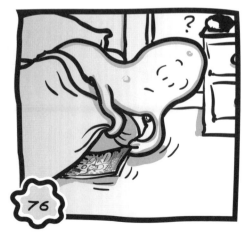

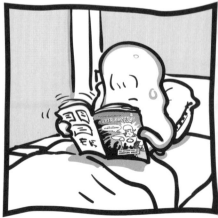

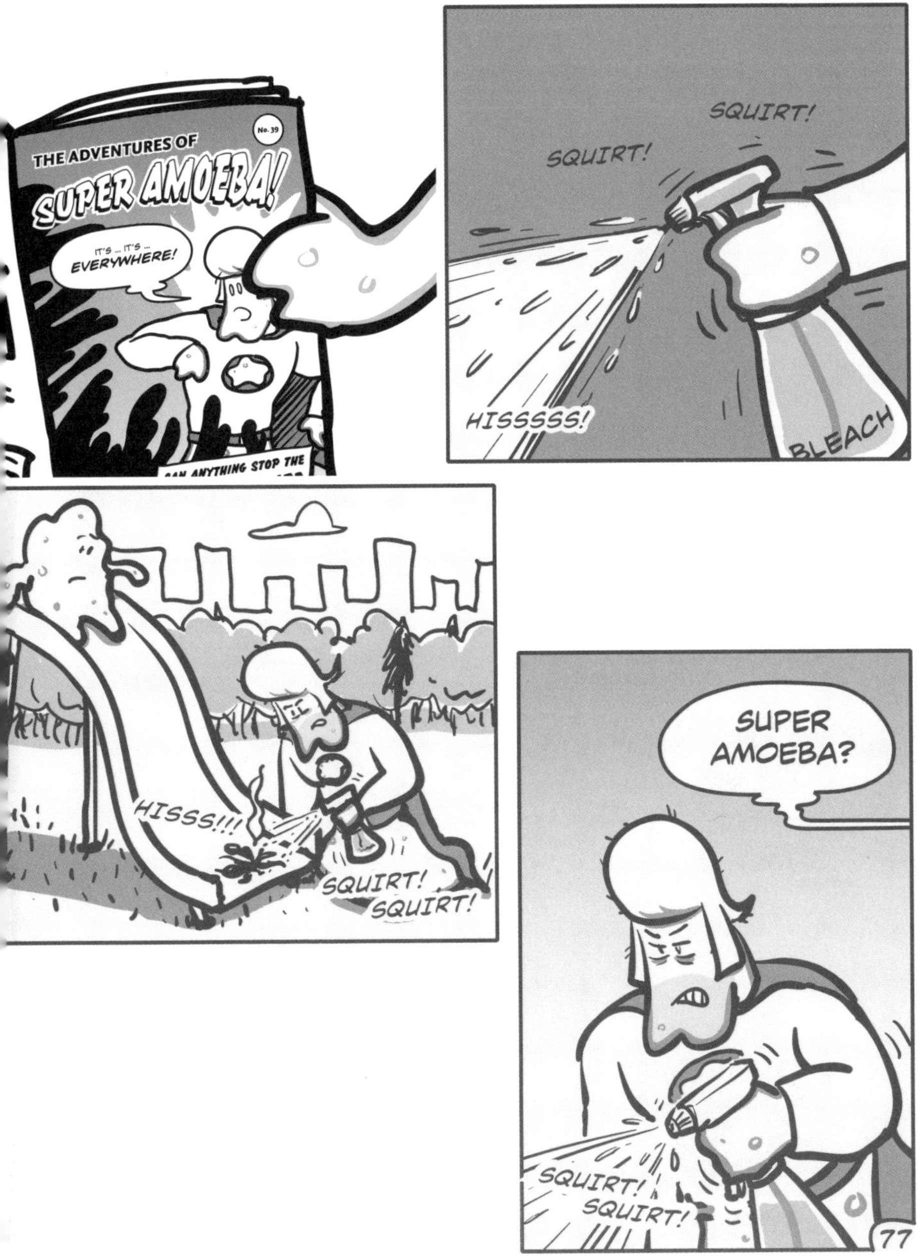
No. 39
THE ADVENTURES OF
SUPER AMOEBA!
IT'S ... IT'S ... EVERYWHERE!
CAN ANYTHING STOP THE
SQUIRT!
SQUIRT!
HISSSSS!
BLEACH
HISSS!!!
SQUIRT!
SQUIRT!
SUPER AMOEBA?
SQUIRT!
SQUIRT!

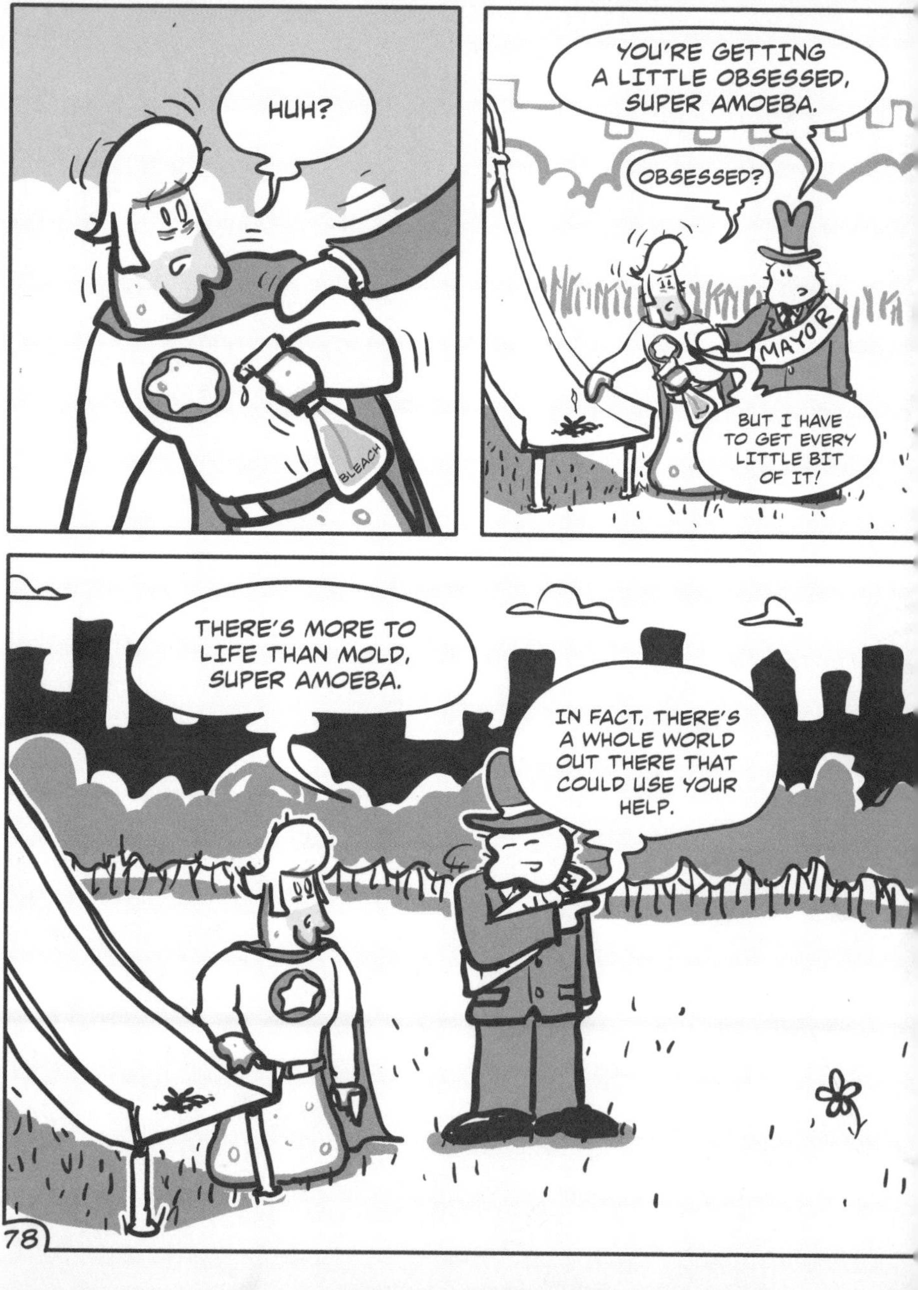
HUH?
BLEACH
YOU'RE GETTING A LITTLE OBSESSED, SUPER AMOEBA.
OBSESSED?
MAYOR
BUT I HAVE TO GET EVERY LITTLE BIT OF IT!
THERE'S MORE TO LIFE THAN MOLD, SUPER AMOEBA.
IN FACT, THERE'S A WHOLE WORLD OUT THERE THAT COULD USE YOUR HELP.

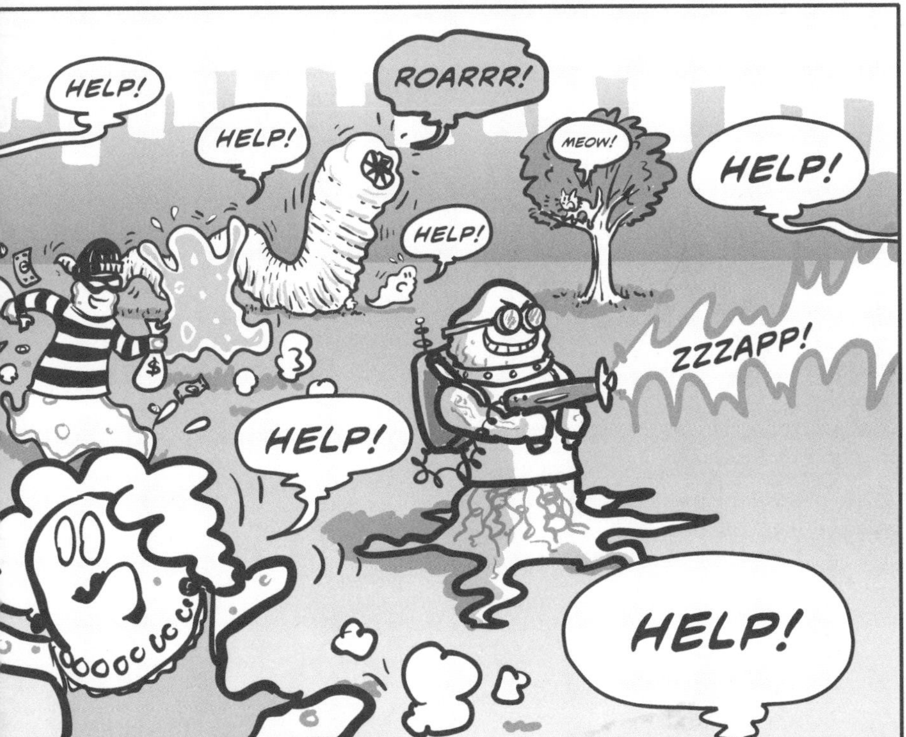
HELP!
HELP!
ROARRR!
MEOW!
HELP!
HELP!
ZZZAPP!
HELP!
HELP!

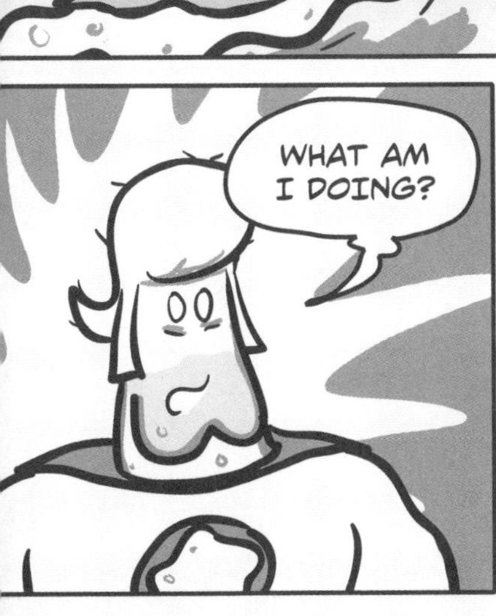
WHAT AM I DOING?

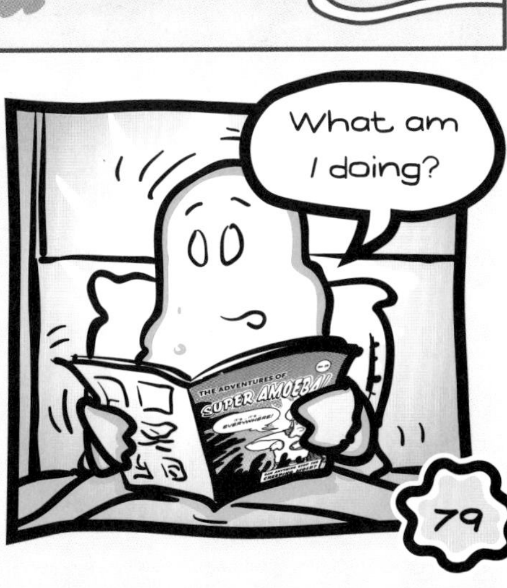
What am I doing?
THE ADVENTURES OF
SUPER AMOEBA!

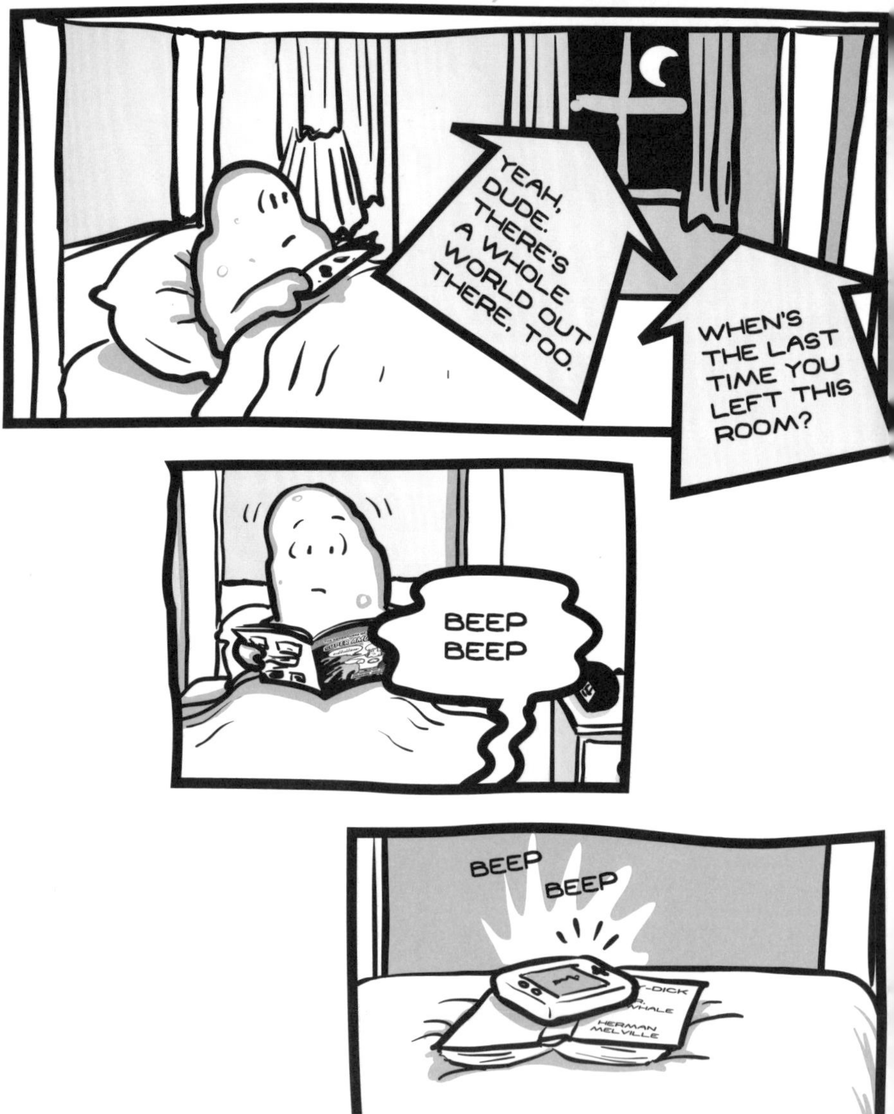
YEAH, DUDE. THERE'S A WHOLE WORLD OUT THERE, TOO.
WHEN'S THE LAST TIME YOU LEFT THIS ROOM?
BEEP BEEP
BEEP
BEEP
HERMAN MELVILLE

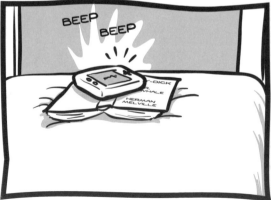

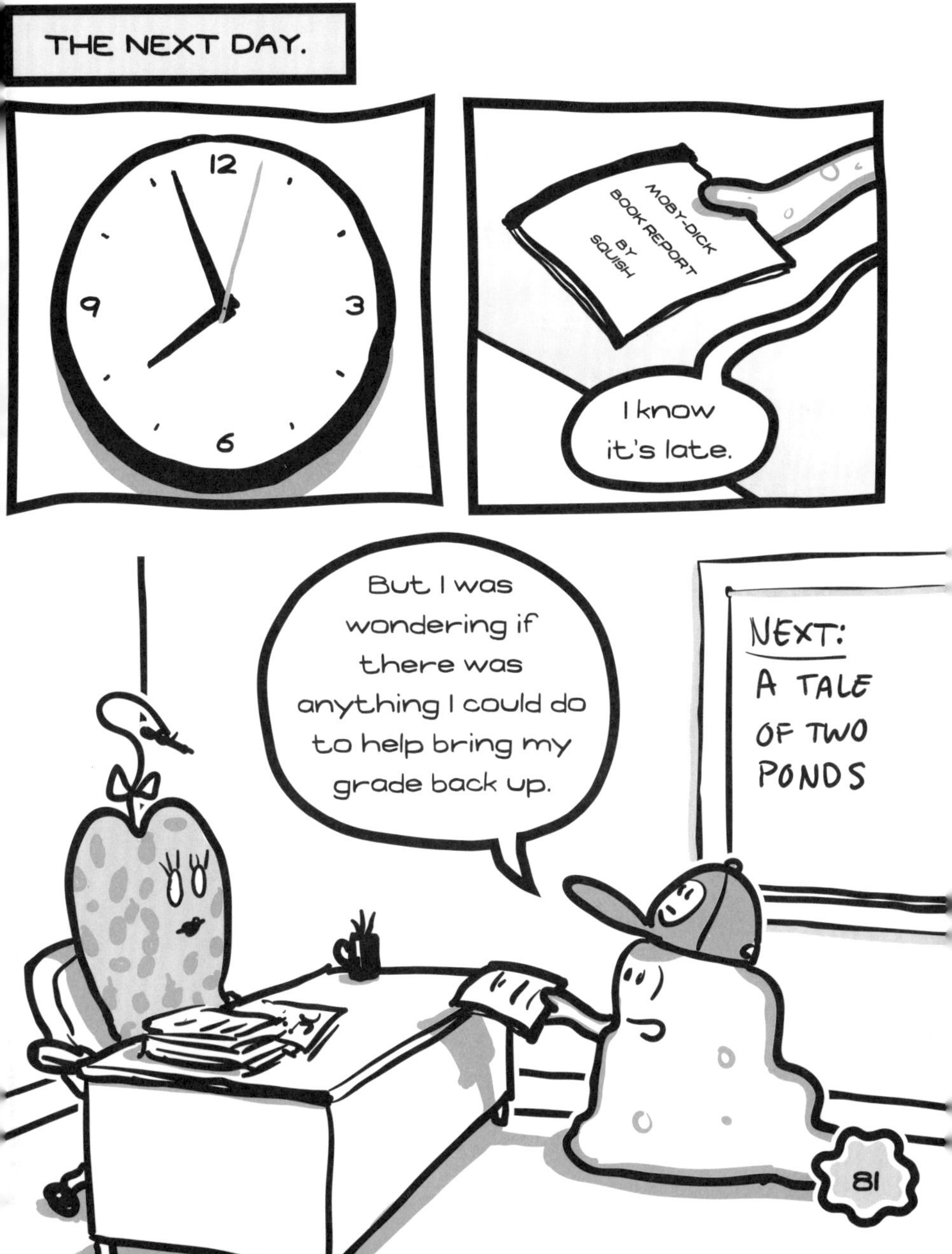
THE NEXT DAY.
12
3
6
9
MOBY-DICK
BOOK REPORT
BY
SQUISH
I know it's late.
But I was wondering if there was anything I could do to help bring my grade back up.
NEXT:
A TALE OF TWO PONDS

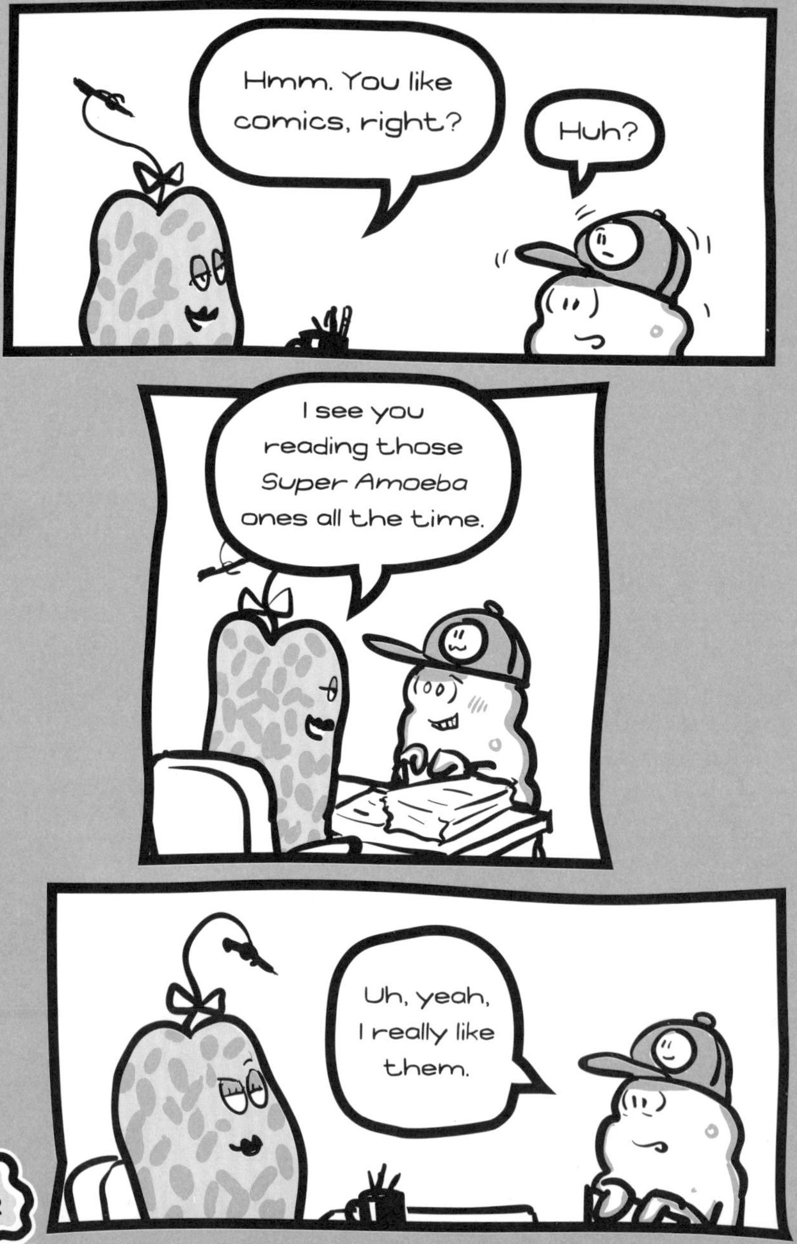
Hmm. You like comics, right?
Huh?
I see you reading those *Super Amoeba* ones all the time.
Uh, yeah, I really like them.

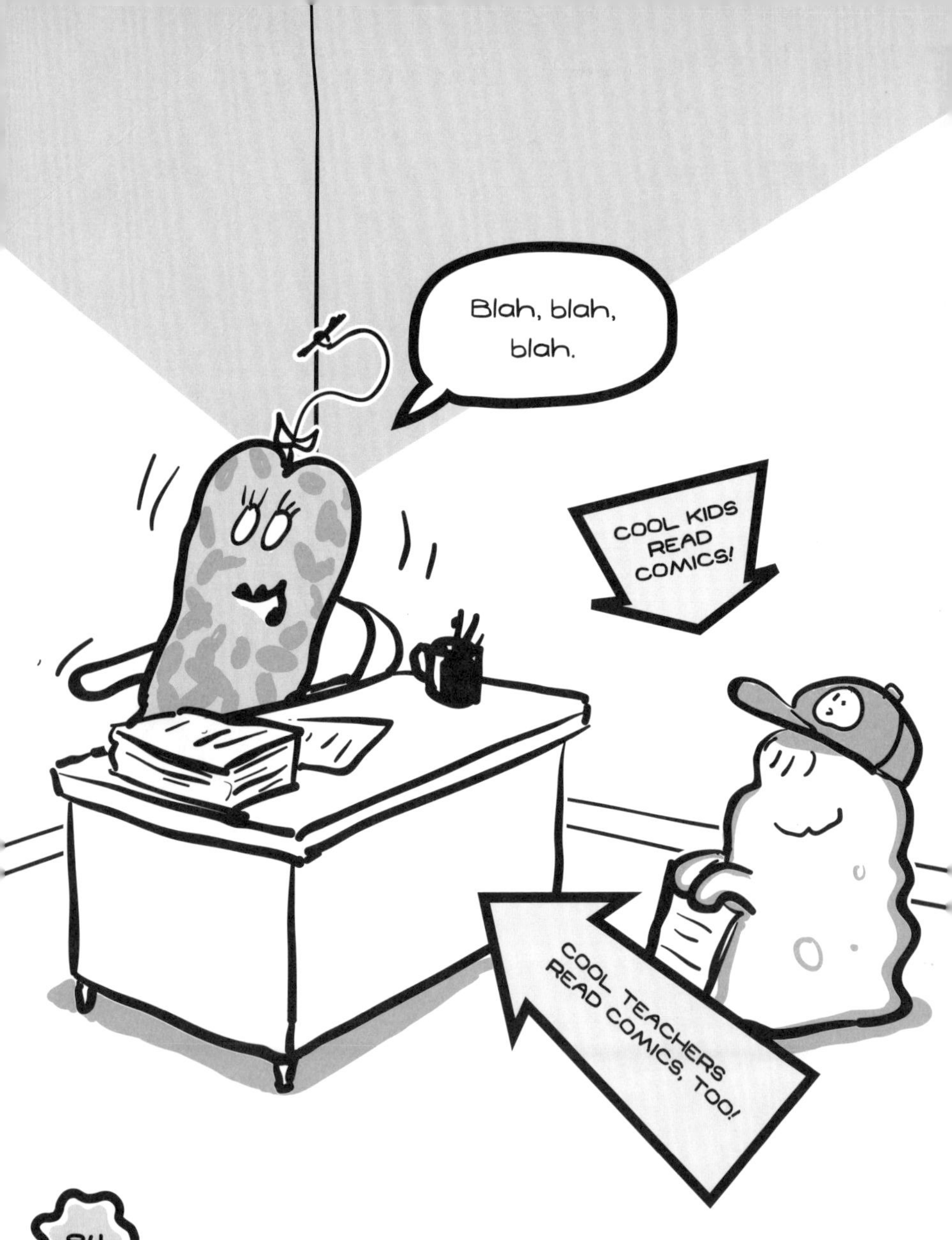
Blah, blah, blah.
COOL KIDS READ COMICS!
COOL TEACHERS READ COMICS, TOO!

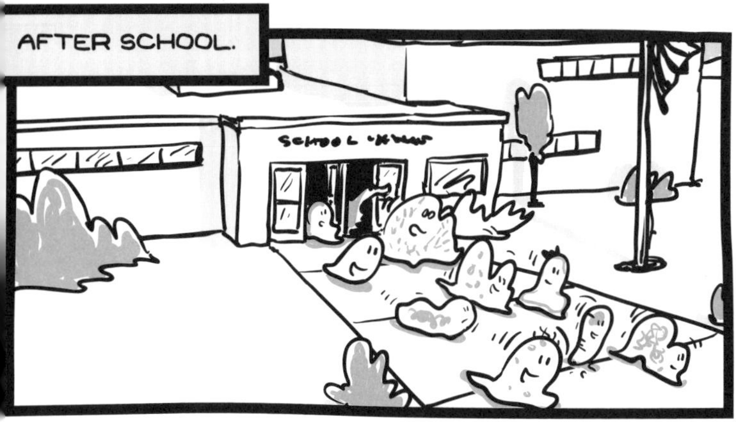
AFTER SCHOOL.

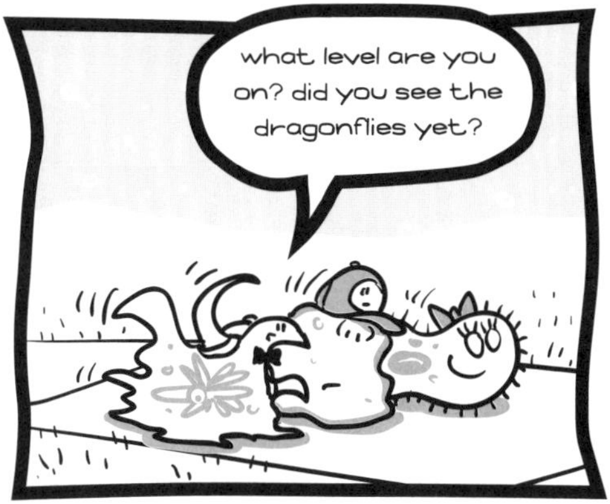
what level are you on? did you see the dragonflies yet?

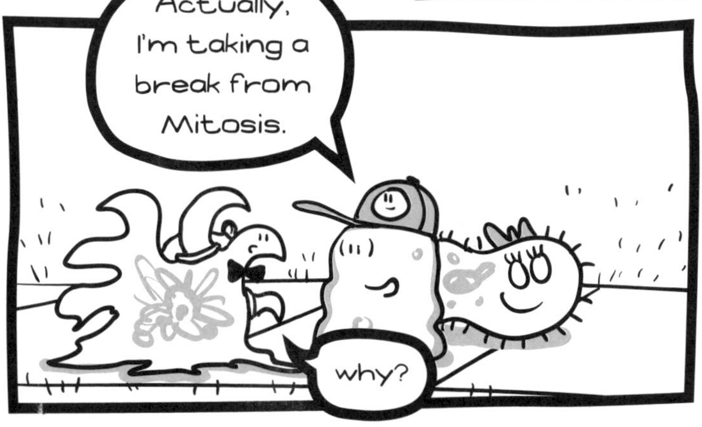
Actually, I'm taking a break from Mitosis.
why?

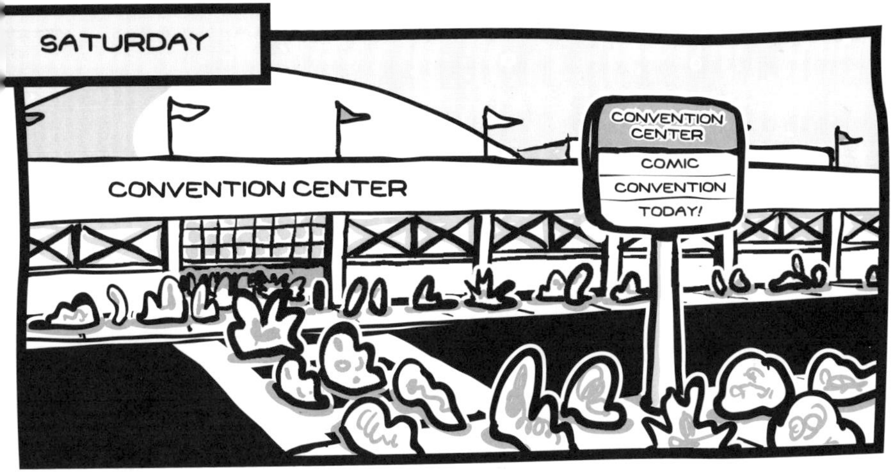
SATURDAY
CONVENTION CENTER
CONVENTION CENTER
COMIC
CONVENTION
TODAY!

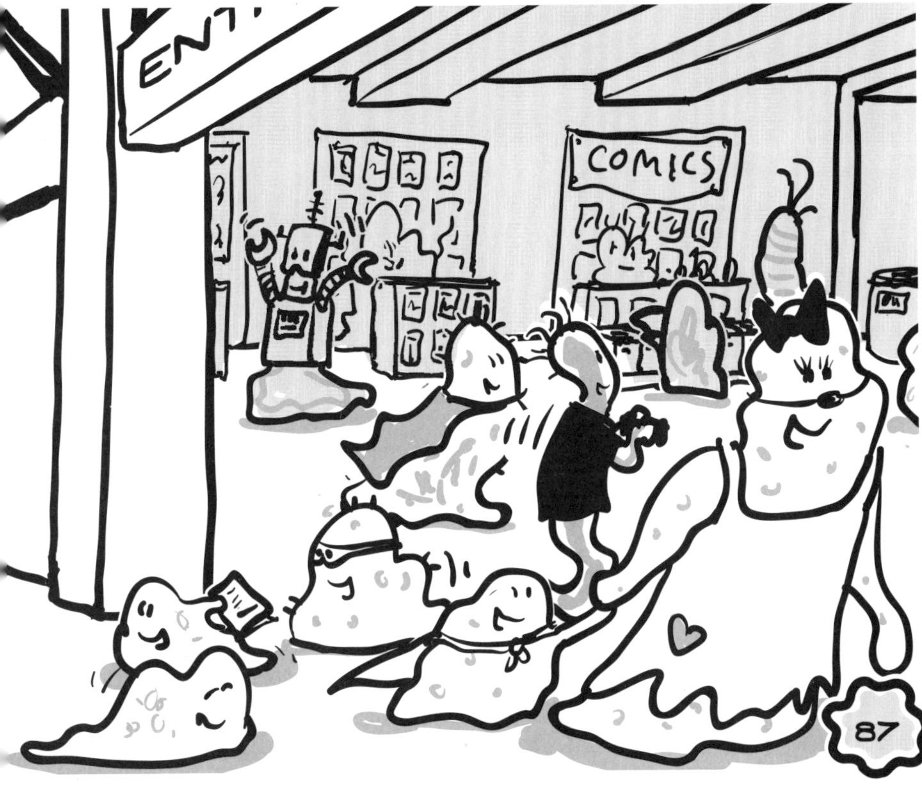
COMICS

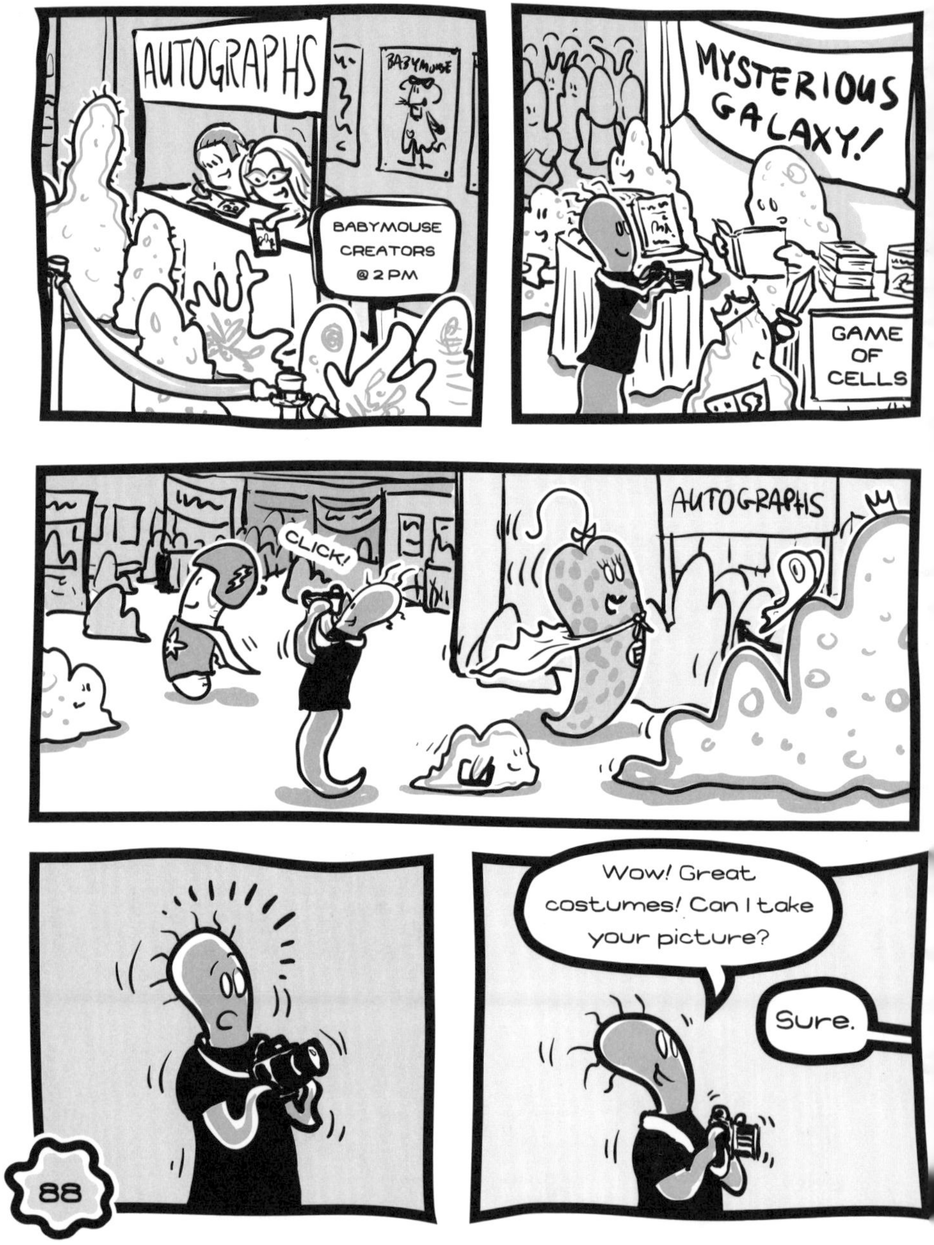
AUTOGRAPHS
BABYMOUSE
BABYMOUSE
CREATORS
@2PM
MYSTERIOUS
GALAXY!
GAME
OF
CELLS
AUTOGRAPHS
CLICK!
Wow! Great
costumes! Can I take
your picture?
Sure.

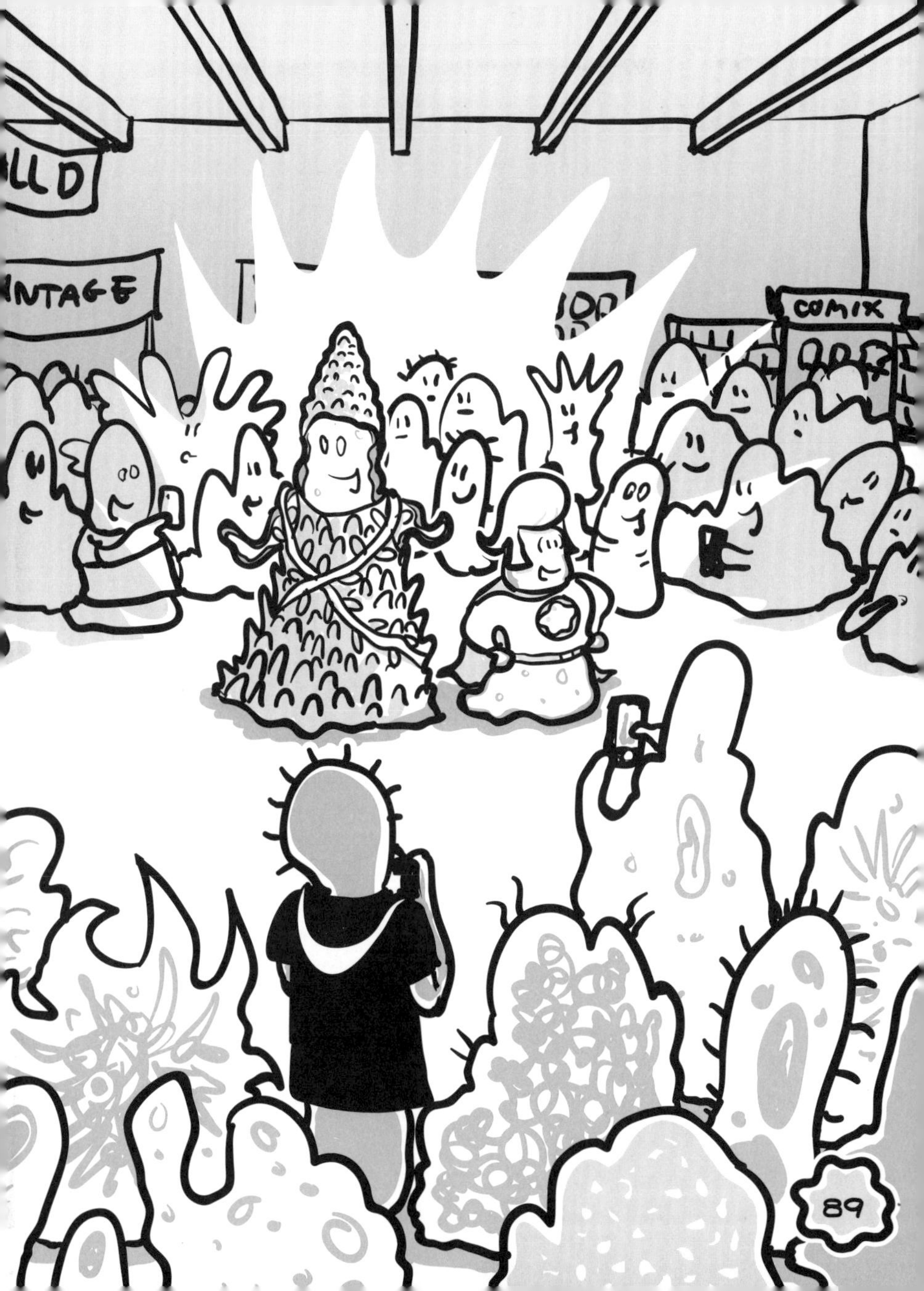
LLD
NTAGE
COMIX

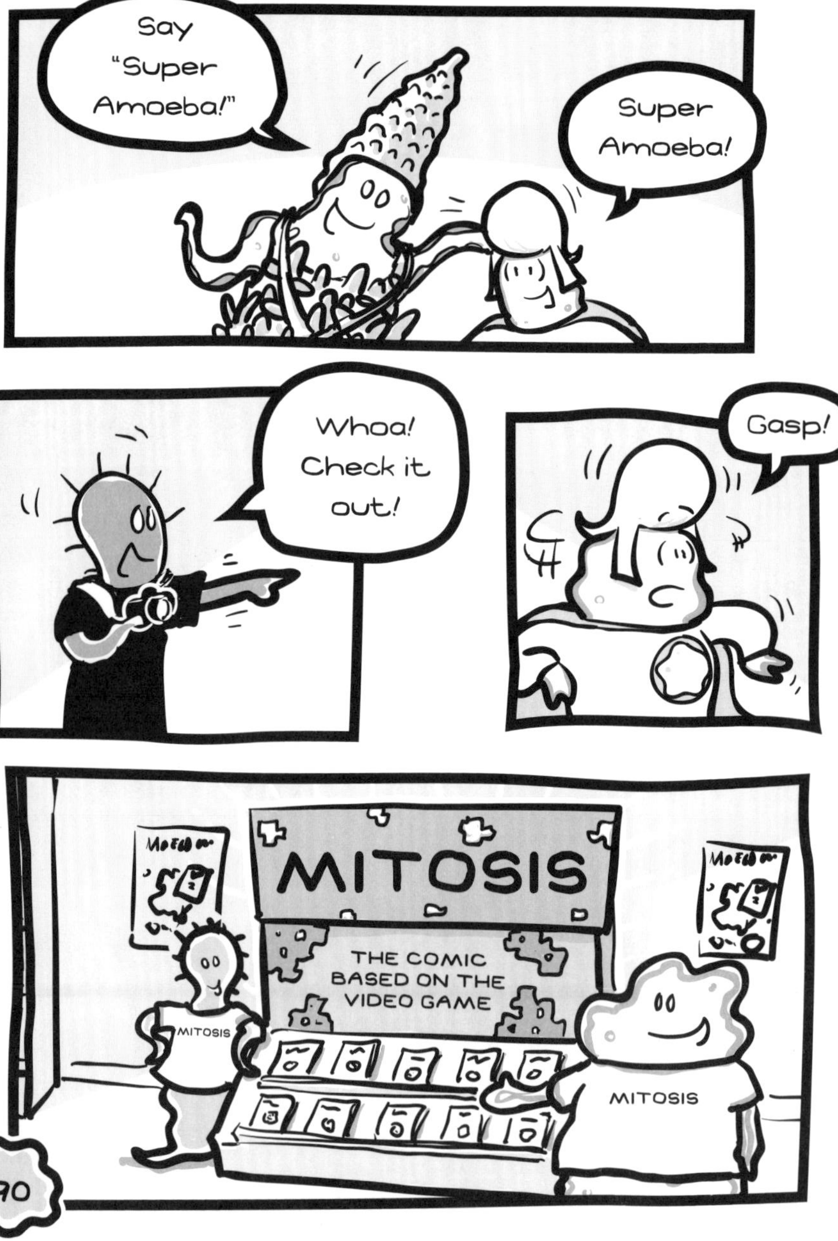
Say "Super Amoeba!"
Super Amoeba!
Whoa! Check it out!
Gasp!
MITOSIS
THE COMIC BASED ON THE VIDEO GAME
MITOSIS
MITOSIS

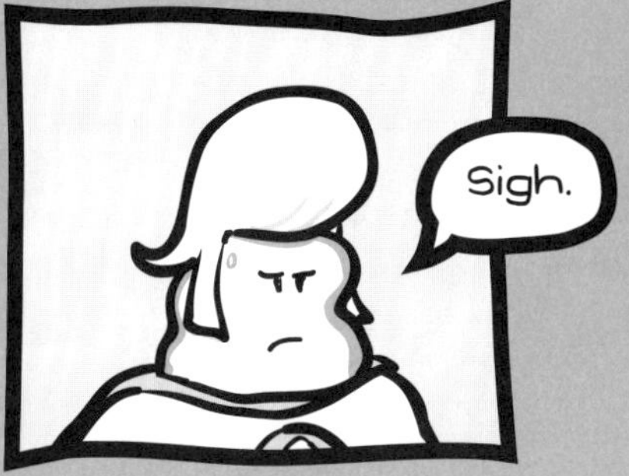
Sigh.

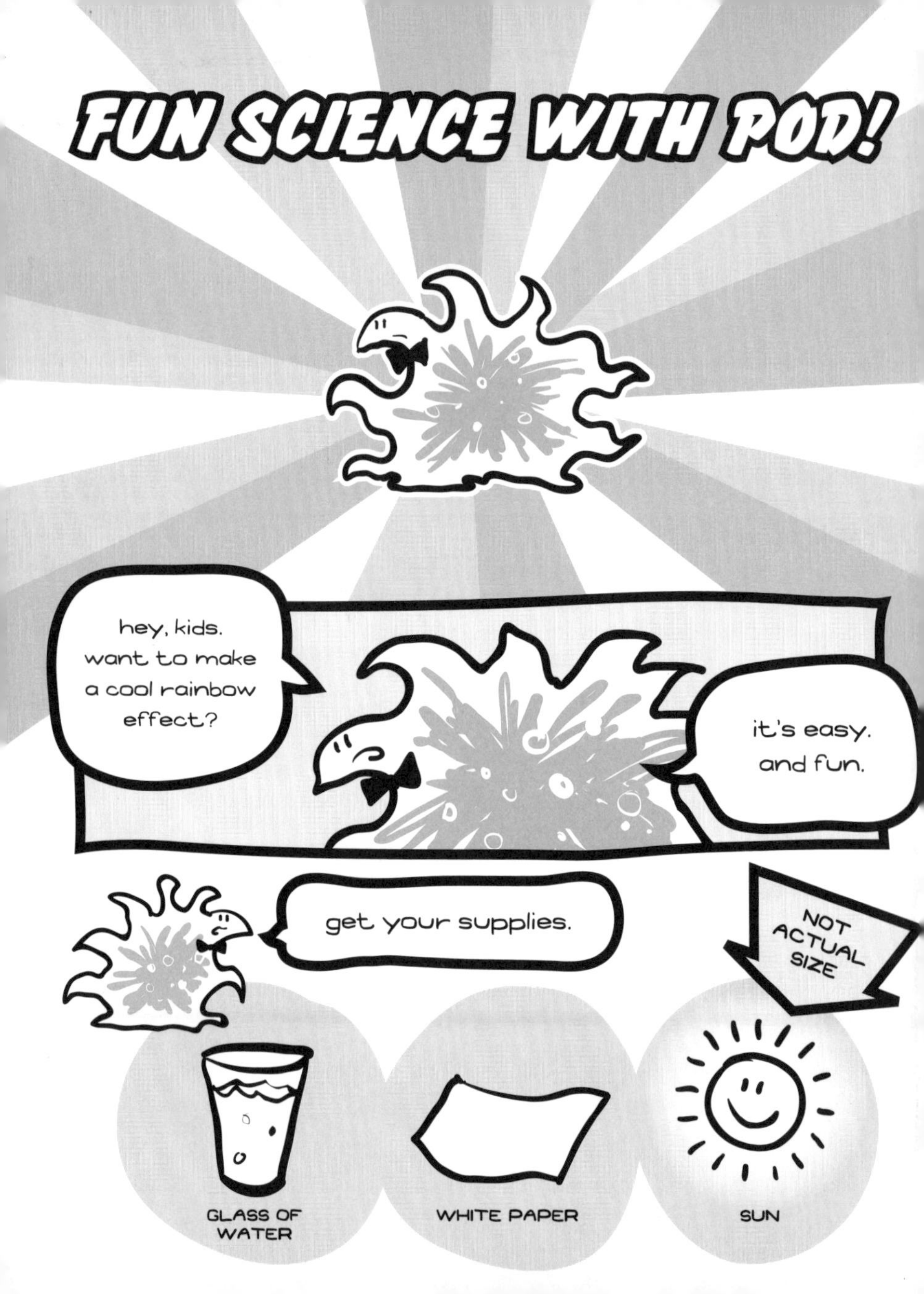
FUN SCIENCE WITH POD!
hey, kids. want to make a cool rainbow effect?
it's easy. and fun.
get your supplies.
NOT ACTUAL SIZE
GLASS OF WATER
WHITE PAPER
SUN

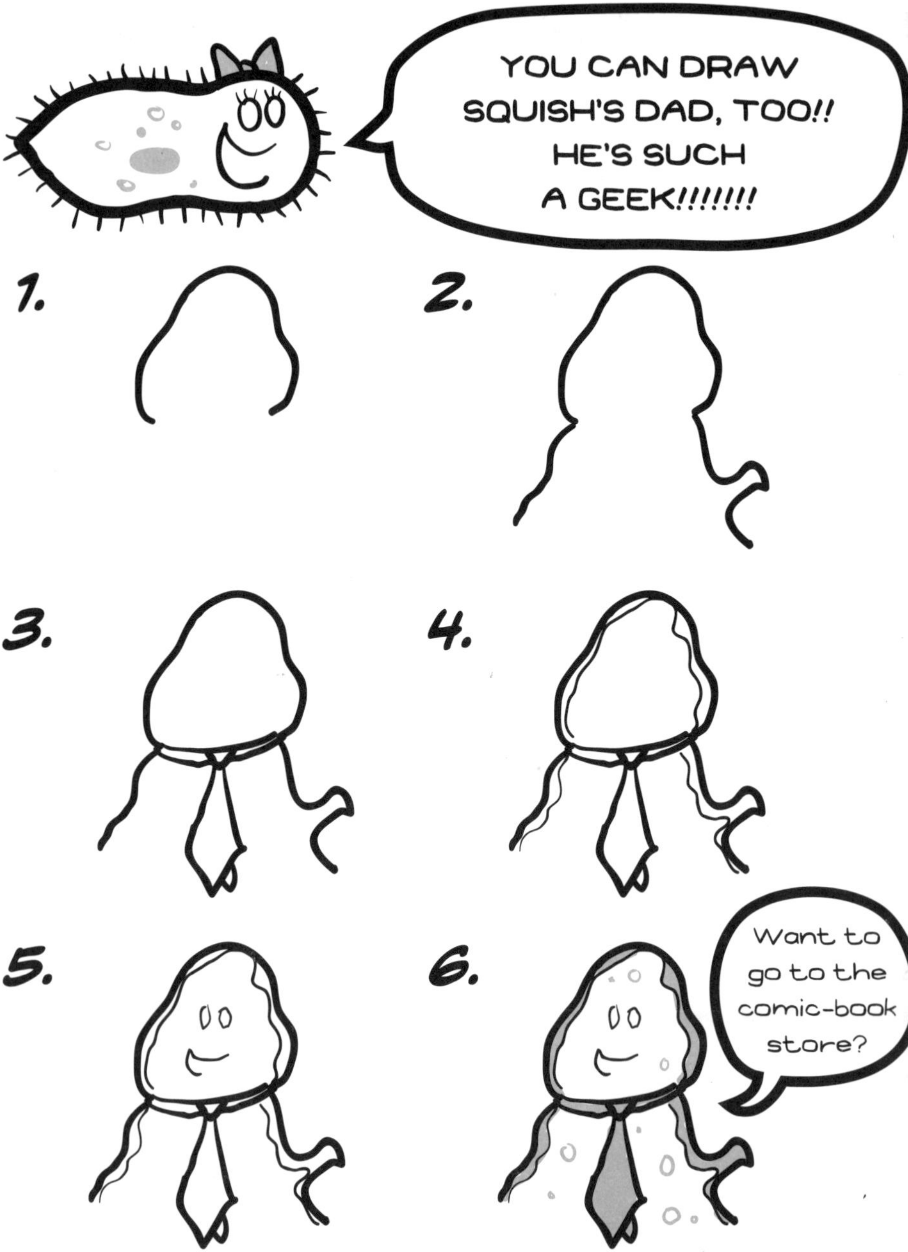
YOU CAN DRAW SQUISH'S DAD, TOO!! HE'S SUCH A GEEK!!!!!!!!
1.
2.
3.
4.
5.
6.
Want to go to the comic-book store?

IF YOU LIKE SQUISH, YOU'LL LOVE BABYMOUSE!

#1 BABYMOUSE: Queen of the World!
#2 BABYMOUSE: Our Hero
#3 BABYMOUSE: Beach Babe
#4 BABYMOUSE: Rock Star
#5 BABYMOUSE: Heartbreaker
#6 CAMP BABYMOUSE
#7 BABYMOUSE: Skater Girl
#8 BABYMOUSE: Puppy Love
#9 BABYMOUSE: Monster Mash
#10 BABYMOUSE: The Musical
#11 BABYMOUSE: Dragonslayer
#12 BABYMOUSE: Burns Rubber
#13 BABYMOUSE: Cupcake Tycoon
#14 BABYMOUSE: Mad Scientist
#15 A Very BABYMOUSE Christmas
#16 BABYMOUSE for President
#17 EXTREME BABYMOUSE

And coming soon:

#18 Happy Birthday, BABYMOUSE

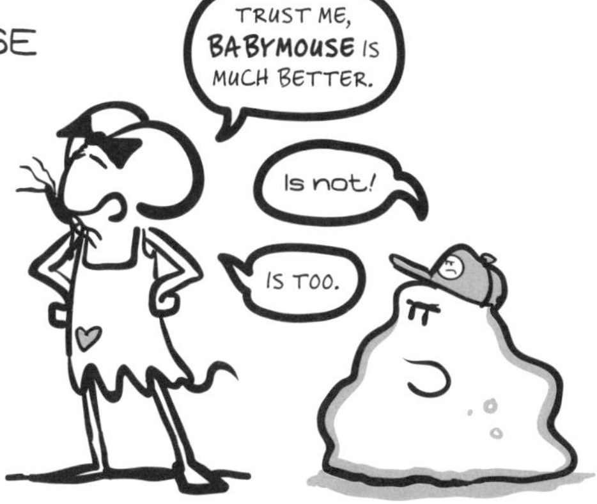
TRUST ME, BABYMOUSE IS MUCH BETTER.
Is not!
IS TOO.

Look for these other great books
by Jennifer L. Holm!

THE BOSTON JANE TRILOGY
EIGHTH GRADE IS MAKING ME SICK
MIDDLE SCHOOL IS WORSE THAN MEATLOAF
OUR ONLY MAY AMELIA
PENNY FROM HEAVEN
TURTLE IN PARADISE